THE CLOSEST OF
FRIENDS

Leslie Harrison

The Closest of Friends by Leslie Harrison

ISBN 978-1-952027-02-4 (Paperback)
ISBN 978-1-952027-03-1 (Hardback)

Printed in the United States of America.

New Leaf Media, LLC
175 S. 3rd Street, Suite 200
Columbus, OH 43215
www.thenewleafmedia.com

CHAPTER 1

Just Another Day

Valentine Frankland was a United States counterterrorism expert who worked alone in Europe finding and neutralizing terrorist cells using whatever means necessary. Now he was using the latest information he had received. To track down and eliminate an eight-man terrorist cell before they could carry out their tasks. The intel he had been given said they were more than likely headed to the United Kingdom— to Scotland. It was feared they were planning to attack the Royal Navy armaments depot at Coulport. So, he had flown to the United Kingdom, rented a car in Glasgow, and driven nearly forty miles north- west towards the naval base at Faslane on Gare Loch, which was about eight miles from the depot. The latest update he had received before he left home was that the attack was imminent. He found a small hotel and booked in. He spent his evenings walking in the area near the base watching for anything unusual. On one of his walks, he found a car parked off the road, he looked around the car and saw noth- ing, he couldn't see anything inside, and the doors were locked. He walked toward the Loch where he found two men with binoculars, Val assumed the glasses would be infrared. They seemed to be studying the depot. They looked to have swarthy complexions, but it was difficult to be certain in the dusk. To Val, they looked Middle Eastern. So, Val stopped to speak to them. "Good evening," he said. "It's a little late for bird watching, but it's a nice night for a walk."

"Get lost," one of the men said.

"Now that's not very friendly," Val said. He frowned appearing hurt.

"You should have stayed home tonight," the other man said.

"Stay home? Why would I have wanted to stay home on such a lovely night?" Val smiled.

"Because now you're going to die," the first man said. He raised a gun fitted with a silencer and pointed it at Val.

The man with the gun turned to his friend and said something Val didn't understand. Then he turned back to Val with the gun still pointed at him. Val moved forward fast. He grabbed hold of the gunman's hand. Val's grip was like a steel trap. He turned the man's hand, so the muzzle of the gun was pointed at the second man. The pressure on the man's wrist caused his finger to jerk and pull the trigger. The bullet hit the second man in the center of the chest. He looked down with a look of almost comical surprise and then crumpled to the ground. The man with the gun tried to pull away from Val's grasp. Val allowed him to pull away slightly, but then Val pulled him back sharply and struck him with an upward blow hard under his nose, driving shards of bone into his brain. The gunman slumped to the ground, twitched a few times, and then lay still. Val bent down and put his fingers on the man's neck under the jaw. No pulse. He was dead; probably had been before he hit the ground. Val walked to the second man. He was still alive—just.

"Help me," the man whispered.

"Yes, of course," Val said not unkindly.

Val pinched the man's nose and covered his mouth. It didn't take long. Val picked up the gun and put it in his pocket. He searched the bodies and found cell phones and passports along with the car keys. He took the keys and walked back to the car. He unlocked it and searched it, finding some papers detailing what the men were planning here and where they were heading next. "Just how dumb are these people?" Val said aloud. He got in and drove to where he had left the dead men. He put them both in the car and drove further up the loch. He got out and put one of the bodies in the driver's seat and buckled him in. Val wiped down everything he had touched. He opened all the windows, put the car in gear, released the parking brake, and let the car roll into the loch. It seemed fitting to let the loch keep their secrets.

With that done, he made his way back to his hotel where he went through the papers and the cell phones he had taken from the men by the loch. He found the names of other members of the cell, and it seemed from the papers that the other cell members were headed for Salisbury in Wiltshire. The following morning, Val checked out of his hotel and drove back to Glasgow Airport. He managed to get a flight to Heathrow Airport where he hired a car and drove to Salisbury. He booked into the Kings Head Hotel and once more went through the papers he had found in Scotland.

According to the papers, Salisbury Cathedral was their target, and the attack was due to happen on Sunday. He had four days to find them. He decided he would park his car and walk to the cathedral. He would visit the cathedral each day, in the morning and evening.

On Friday morning, as he was leaving, he passed two men who were going in. He waited outside for the men to come out, and when they did, he followed them and watched them get into a van and drive away. Val went back to the cathedral; he looked around but found nothing. He came back on Saturday morning and saw nothing; he returned for another visit in the evening. This time, as he stood outside the building, he saw the same two men he had seen on Friday. Val went inside and searched the inside of the cathedral. Under the pulpit, he found a small case. When he opened it, he found enough explosives connected to a cell phone to level the entire cathedral. Val disconnected the cell phone. He closed the case, picked it up, and walked outside. He looked around and saw the van the two men had gotten into on Friday. He walked to the van, opened the passenger door, and got in. The two men looked at him and then at the gun he held in his hand.

The driver held up a cell phone. "You're too late," he said, and he pressed the call button.

Val held up the small case. "Too bad," he said.

The two men looked at each other.

"Don't think about it," Val said. "Keep still and do as I say. Now, I want you to start the engine and drive."

"Where too?" the driver asked sullenly.

"Don't worry. I'll give you directions as we go. And drive within the speed limits. Don't try anything stupid."

They set off and drove. Val directed them out of town and to a remote spot on the Salisbury Plain where he made them stop. Val ordered the driver to turn off the engine. He took the keys and made them get into the back of the van. He got in with them.

"What do you want?" one of the men asked.

"I want us to have a conversation. You can tell me where your friends are and what they are planning to do."

"Fuck yourself, Englishman," said the man who had been driving.

"Englishman?" Val said, his eyebrows raised.

"We are willing to die for what we believe," said the other man.

"Yes, of course, seventy-two virgins and rivers of honey. Well, don't let me hold you up," Val said. He shot both men through the heart.

Val searched both bodies and the van. Once more he found passports, cell phones, and papers listing targets. Val opened the case and re-attached the cell phone to the explosives. He got out of the van and walked away. When he was far enough away, he pressed the call button on the cell phone. There was a bright flash then a large boom. Val smiled. When the police arrived, they would conclude that the men were making a bomb and blew themselves up. He set off walking back to his hotel. It would be a long walk, but he didn't mind; in fact, he would enjoy the walk.

When Val got back to his hotel, he began to look through all the papers and maps he had taken from the van. From what he could make out, it seemed that the Mall of Berlin in Germany was most likely the next target. Also, there was an address in Kreuzburg, a district of Berlin that wasn't far from the mall. It was a place he knew. He had been there before when he had been looking for persons of interest. He packed his things and checked out. He had taken the gun apart, and he disposed of the pieces in drains and waste bins as he walked to his car.

He drove back to the airport where he used his not inconsiderable charm on the customer service assistant to get a cancellation seat on the next flight to Berlin. After an uneventful flight, he rented a car and found a hotel. Then he went to visit someone he knew who would sell him what he needed. He bought a gun—a Glock 17 with a silencer— plus fifty rounds of ammunition. He bought a map and drove to the address that was in the papers he had brought from England. He began to watch the house. Once he was sure the four men he wanted were inside, he picked up a cardboard box. Earlier he had cut a hole in the side of the box. Now he grabbed the gun and slid it into the box. Still holding the gun, now concealed in the box, he walked to the front door. He rang the bell and waited. He heard the door being unlocked. Then it opened a crack, and a face peered out. "What do you want?" the man said.

"I have a delivery for you," Val said.

"You have the wrong address."

"I don't think so," Val said, and he pushed the door open.

The man started to raise a gun, but Val used his left hand to strike him in the throat and pushed him out of the way, leaving him to strangle in his blood. Another face appeared. Val raised the box and pulled the trigger. The box blew apart as did the face of the man in front of Val. As Val pushed forward, two more men confronted him. Val's gun spits twice more, the sound like a muffled bang, then there was silence. Val searched the house; there was no one else there. Val moved the bodies to make it look as if they had quarreled and fought to kill each other. He doubted that the police would believe it, but there was no way they would get within a mile of the truth. He checked things one more time then left the house. He went back to his hotel. He decided to stay in Berlin for a few days before going home—a bit of rest.

When Val finally returned to his apartment in Paris feeling rested and refreshed his, he called into his control to report that his mission had been a success, all of the threats had been neutralized. Once he had completed his report, he was told that he was being recalled to Washington to deal with a domestic issue. A room had been reserved for him in a small but comfortable hotel on the edge of the city. He was told to check in, sit tight, and wait for further orders. Val hung up, he frowned at the phone, obviously annoyed.

Val brooded for a while, then he called the airline and booked a flight. The following day Val flew back to Washington, once there he took a cab and went to the designated hotel, he checked in, he went up to his room. Closed the behind him and sat on the bed. "*What the fuck am I doing here.*" He thought. Val took a shower then went to bed. The following morning, he went out for his morning run in a nearby park. When he returned to the hotel, the receptionist told him there was a message for him. He took the envelope, said thank you, and returned to his room once there he read the orders, he threw the slip of paper on to the bed. He showered dried himself then re-read the orders.

For the attention of Mr. V. Frankland:

You are ordered to report to Special Agent Thomes at his office on Monday morning at 07:00 hours as instructed, there is a domestic issue that requires your attention. You will receive a full briefing upon arrival.

Regards

D. Thomes

This didn't make any sense to him. He was doing his job—a job he had asked to do, granted, but he was doing it and doing it well. And now they called him back home to deal with a domestic issue.

"What the fuck is a domestic issue?" Val said aloud. "And why the fuck do they need me to deal with it? Don't they have people here who can deal with this…whatever this is? Or if this is just a domestic problem, surely they could use the local police?"

And just why the fuck did Thomes want him to come back anyway? That just didn't make any sense at all. Special Agent Dexter Thomes *hated* having Val around. The last time Val had been in Washington, Thomes had said he wanted to stand Val against a wall and shoot him. Now he wanted him back.

"Perhaps he's finally gotten permission to put me against that wall," Val said, again out loud, and he laughed to himself.

When Val and Thomes were young and just starting in their careers, they used to joke that, when the revolution came, they would be the first against the wall. Val smiled despite himself. He supposed he had better find out what Thomes wanted. After all, what else was he going to do? He supposed he could sit there and drink, but maybe that wasn't such a great idea. Besides, despite everything, it would be good to see Thomes and the rest of the old gang again—or what remained of the old gang. It had been a long time since he'd been home.

Val got ready and made his way to the office block in Farragut Square where Thomes and his team had their headquarters. When he got there, he stood outside just looking at the large glass edifice. He didn't know what he expected to feel when he got there, but he felt nothing; it was just a building.

+++

Inside this building, Ricardo Belin, Susanne Wilder, and Benny Ferral, all of them Agent Thomes's main team of field agents, were laughing and joking and talking about what they had been up to over the weekend. Ricardo and Susanne were good-naturedly teasing Benny because he had spent the weekend at a role-playing game convention.

"So, what have you two been doing?" Benny asked.

Susanne said she had spent a quiet weekend just watching movies and eating chocolates.

"I told you that you should have come with me," Ricardo said to her. He was always asking her out, but she always declined.

"No, thank you. Sitting watching men play with their balls is not what I call a good time," Susanne said.

"We could have done other things," Ricardo said. "We could have gone for drinks, maybe dancing, or nice quiet dinner," He said.

"Maybe another time," Susanne said, without looking at him.

The three of them carried on with their conversations unaware of how their lives were going to change very soon.

+++

Val felt no sense of excitement or foreboding at being back at the old headquarters. People passing by him on the street looked at him. He was a good-looking young man—six feet tall, medium build, brown wavy hair. He just stood there looking at the building. He guessed people thought that maybe he was a bit slow, or maybe he was just into architecture. Either way, everyone was giving him a wide berth.

Very slowly, Val realized that people were giving him odd looks. Val laughed to himself. He supposed he had better get moving before someone thought to call the cops—or maybe the guys in the white coats who were armed with the jackets that fastened up the back and the injections that made you feel all happy and relaxed.

He laughed at himself again, and people stared at him. He started walking towards the office block.

As he walked through the main door, he noticed that the security guards were watching him very closely. They must have seen him standing outside and were keeping an eye on him as he passed through the metal detectors and made his way to the reception desk.

The young woman sitting behind the desk looked him up and down then smiled at him. "Good morning, sir," she said. "And how may I help you today?"

He smiled back at her. "And a good morning to you as well," he said. "I have an appointment to see Special Agent Thomes."

"Could I have your name please, sir?" the receptionist asked.

"Yes, of course," Val said. "My name is Val Frankland, and I received this cable." He showed her the letter telling him where to report.

"Thank you," she said. "Please sign in and take this visitor's pass and this piece of paper." She held these things in her hand.

"What's this?" he asked.

She smiled. "That's my phone number. In case you get lost. If you need helping to find Agent Thomes's office, just give me a call. And if you like I can be searched and you can be rescued."

Val smiled back at her. "Thank you very much." He looked at her name badge. "Kyra, that is very kind of you. I think I can find Agent Thomes's office myself, but I will keep this safe just in case."

"Yes," she said. "Please do. Don't hesitate to call me anytime."

He smiled at her. "Thanks." He extended his hand and she reached out and took it. He bent from the waist and kissed the back of her hand. "I'll call you later," he said.

"I'll look forward to it," she said, smiling.

Val smiled back. "Yeah, me too."

Val made his way to the elevators. As he walked he felt an itch in his spine, he turned around to see Kyra watching him. She waggled her fingers at him in a wave. He waved back and entered the elevator.

He rode up to the seventh floor. The route to Thomes's offices had never failed to amuse him. He had come up seven floors and now he had to go down six floors to get where he wanted to be. This, he knew, was because of the fact they sometimes held suspects in the cells. The location and route made it more difficult for any of them to escape.

He got out of the second elevator and made his way to Thomes's office. As he approached the squad room, he saw that it hadn't changed since he was there the last time. It was still the horrible green color he had always hated. Thomes's office was still at the far end of the room, and there were still five desks, three on one side a two on the other. Val thought back to when he had been there before. As he stood outside the glass walls, he could see himself with his old friends laughing and joking. With an effort, he shook himself and returned to the now.

When Val looked again, he saw two men and a woman standing by their desks. They were all looking at him. They had all seen Val approach the squad room, and they had watched him as he had just stopped and stood there staring into space.

+++

The three agents, Ricardo, Susanne, and Benny all looked at each other and then back at Val. They saw him shake his head as if to clear it. He looked around and then began to walk towards them. Ricardo stood and walked forward to meet him. Although Ricardo was at least four inches taller than the man and he outweighed him by at least fifty pounds, there was something about this man. For some reason he couldn't put his finger on, Ricardo felt intimidated by him. He could not have said why. He just did.

"Good morning," Ricardo said. "Can I help you?" he asked, smiling.

"Good morning," the man replied. "And, yes, maybe you can help me. My name is Val Frankland, and I received orders to report to special Agent Dexter Thomes here at zero seven hundred this morning."

Ricardo held out his hand. "May I see your orders?" he asked.

"My orders stated that I should report to Agent Thomes, and you are not Agent Thomes, are you?" Val said.

"No, I am not, but when Agent Thomes isn't here, I am in charge."

Val looked Ricardo up and down. "Things must be desperate," he said.

Ricardo glared at him. "And what is that supposed to mean?"

"Never mind. But I still want to see Agent Thomes."

"I'm sorry, but I'm afraid that Agent Thomes isn't here right now," Ricardo said. He was doing his best to be polite, but he was boiling up inside. "He's usually here by this time, so he must have been held up. But seeing as you don't want to give me your papers, maybe you can tell me what you are here for. Then maybe I can help you."

"Yes," Val said. "Maybe you could, but it would be of more use if you could find out when Agent Thomes will be here."

"I've already told you I don't know. If Agent Thomes has been held up, I don't know when he will get here," Ricardo said. He was not a very patient man, and he was becoming angrier by the minute with this arrogant son of a bitch.

"Yes, you have," Val said. "Can't you call him to find out where he is?"

"I'm sorry," Ricardo said. "I can't do that, and if you knew Special Agent Thomes you would know that you don't just call him up and ask him where he is, and what he's doing. So, I have no intention of calling him to ask him where he is, but if you would like to leave a contact number and a message, I will see that Agent Thomes gets it. I'll ask him to get back to you as soon as possible."

"I do know Agent Thomes, and I don't want to leave a message. I have an appointment to meet with Agent Thomes here this morning. Now, if you will excuse me, I'll wait in Thomes's office."

Val began to walk forward, and Ricardo put a hand on his arm to restrain him. Val looked down at Ricardo's hand and then back up to his face. "Now are you sure you have no more use for that hand?"

Ricardo looked at him. "And just what the hell is that supposed to mean?"

"It means that, if you don't remove your hand from my arm, I will remove it for you. I'll rip it off
and shove it so far up your ass, you'll be able to brush your teeth from the inside."

Ricardo looked at the man, disbelief showing on his face. "What did you say?"

"What? Are you deaf as well as stupid?" Val replied.

Ricardo was stopped from answering by Melanie, a small dark-haired woman with lively, intelligent eyes who had a penchant for short skirts, came into the room with a question on her face. But then she saw Val, and her dark eyes lit up with joy. Ricardo was surprised as she ran to him with a squeal of delight. He felt a sudden burst of hatred for this man, this Val Frankland. Just who the hell was he? Melanie never treated *him* this way. She wasn't cold towards him, but he never felt that she liked him this much.

She threw her arms around Val's neck and gave him a big hug and a kiss. Val lifted her off her feet and swung her around easily as if she were a child. "Wow," Val said. "Now that's what I call a greeting."

"It's just so good to see you!" she said as she gave him another hug. "It's been so long."

"Yes, it has," Val agreed. "It's been far too long."

Ricardo watched Melanie with the man who had introduced himself as Val Frankland. "I take it you two know each other?" he said.

"Of course, we do," Melanie said. "And I hope that is the last stupid question you're going to ask today. Do you see me doing this with everyone who comes here?" She had a big smile on her face.

"So, who are you?" Ricardo asked.

"I've told you my name. Apart from that, you don't need to know who I am," Val said.

Susanne and Benny walked forward to join the others. Susanne Wilder was five foot five and had strawberry blond hair; in fact, she looked like a model. She was a member of Thomes's team as an exceptional artist. She had previously worked freelance, mainly with the local police as a sketch artist. She was very good at what she did. While she worked with people to get descriptions of persons of interest, she could put them at ease and get the best out of them. Thomes had met her through the police department when she did some sketches for him of some people he was looking for. As soon as Thomes had seen how good she was and how she worked, he had offered her a job on his team as an investigator and sketch artist. Susanne had thought the job sounded interesting, so she'd agreed.

Benny Ferral had been recruited fresh from college. He had graduated with a double doctorate from MIT. He was an absolute wizard with any kind of electronic device. Thomes quickly saw the advantage of having Benny as part of the team, so he had talked Benny into joining up.

The man who had introduced himself as Val Frankland stood with his arm around Melanie's shoulders. He was six feet tall, with an even tan, he had light brown hair and blue eyes. Ricardo saw the way Susanne was looking at Val and the way Val was noticing Susanne; he was not happy about it.

+++

Val had noticed Susanne. He couldn't help it. She looked quite a bit like his late wife. She did not look exactly like her, but she could have been her sister. He felt something he had not felt in a long time. When he looked at her, his stomach felt like a basket of writhing snakes. He was trying not to make it obvious that he was looking, but he was watching her just the same, thinking how beautiful she was, wondering what it would be like to run his fingers through her hair and hold her and kiss her. *Stop this*, he told himself. *You have enough problems without adding more. Just keep your mind on what you are here for.* Then part of his mind asked. *Oh yeah? And just why are you here? What are you supposed to do here? Just what the hell is the domestic issue?* Those were questions he would get the answers to soon enough when Thomes got there. Then he would find out why the hell Thomes had sent for him. His mind kept returning to this young woman who had attracted him, and he found there was nothing he could do about it. He suddenly realized that Melanie was speaking to him. "Sorry," he said. "I was miles away."

"That's okay. I was just saying that this is a wonderful surprise, but what are you doing here?"

Val shrugged. "I'm not exactly sure. I just received orders to report to Thomes here this morning, so here I am."

"Yes, here you are. It does seem strange that he would have you recalled. Do you think he might have forgiven you? And he will be happy to see you?"

Val smiled. "You never know with Thomes. He was pissed at me for leaving here and taking this job working in Europe."

"Well, I'm happy to see you," Melanie said. "And I'm sure that Doc will be as well. Maybe we could go for a drink later."

Val smiled again. "That sounds like a good idea. It sure is good to know that there is someone here who is happy to see me. While I was on my way here, I wondered if maybe I should have worn some thermals just in case I got a frosty reception, and maybe body armor just in case Thomes decides he does want to shoot me after all." He laughed. "I still can't understand why he would ask me to come back, not after the last time. If I remember, he said I was stupid for doing what I was going to do and that he would like to put me against the wall and shoot me himself before someone else could do it."

"So, Melanie aren't you going to introduce us to your friend?" Ricardo asked.

"No, she is not," said Thomes as he entered the squad room.

Val turned to face Thomes. He was tall and broad-shouldered with jet black hair and an angular handsome face; his hair was always neatly combed, and as always, he was wearing a shirt and tie.

"Good morning and fuck you too, Dex," Val said.

"So, you managed to find your way back here I see, and I've told you before not to call me Dex."

"Yeah, well, I thought I had better get on over here. Your letter made it sound as if you needed me," Val said.

"I need you like I need a hole in my head," Thomes snapped at him.

"Maybe you shouldn't have sent for me then," Val replied.

"It wasn't all my idea, trust me." Thomes snapped back.

"Well, it says here that it was. The orders are signed by you. But I don't understand why you wanted me to come back."

"It states in your orders why you were called back."

Val laughed. "A domestic issue it says. Why the hell do you need me for a domestic issue? What does that even mean?" Val waved his arm towards Thomes's team. "Why do you even have these people here if you can't deal with a domestic issue?"

The other members of the team stood watching this exchange with interest; they had never heard anyone speak to Thomes that way before.

+++

Just then Director Trena Kennedy came into the squad room. "Good morning, Val," she said. "I'm sorry I'm late. I had to call for a briefing, and it took a little longer than I expected."

Val turned to look at her. "Hello, Trena. Yes, it has been a long time. Don't worry about it. You know me—I always like to be the early bird. Thomes and his team have been keeping me entertained."

"You never change, do you?" she said.

"No, I don't suppose I do. But then, if I changed, you wouldn't love me anymore, would you?"

"If the two of you have finished with the double comedy act ..." said Thomes.

"Sorry, Agent Thomes," Val said.

"We will continue this discussion in my office," said the director. "Now both of you follow me." She turned and walked in the direction of her office.

Thomes turned to the rest of the team who had been standing around watching what was happening. "Don't you guys have any work to do? If you don't, I can certainly find you some."

They all went back to their desks. Val looked at Melanie. He smiled and winked. "I'll see you later ..."

"If we're spared," she finished for him.

He turned and followed Thomes to Trena's office.

+++

"Just who does he think he is?" Ricardo said.

"What do you mean?" Melanie asked.

"Him!" Ricardo said. "What an arrogant son of a bitch he is. If you hadn't come in when you did ..."

"If I hadn't come in when I did, he would have put you in traction at the very least. Trust me. I know him."

"So, who is he then?" Ricardo asked.

"No one you would want to mess with—that is something I can tell you. As for anything else you want to know, you will have to ask him—or Thomes—when they get back."

"Yeah, well, he doesn't scare me," Ricardo said.

"I don't think for one minute he was trying to scare you. But, as I said, if you mix it up with him, you are a fool. He will chew you up and spit you out."

Ricardo just looked at her.

"Is he that good?" Susanne asked.

"Yes," Melanie said. "He is that good." Melanie looked at Ricardo. "What's your best score on the assault course?"

"Why?" he asked.

"What is your best score?" she asked again.

"I got eighty-five percent last time. Why?"

"Well, the last time I saw Val do the assault course, he scored ninety-nine-point five percent, and he was having a bad day. That should give you some idea of how good he is."

"Wow, that *is* good," Susanne said.

"Maybe it was a one-off, or maybe he was just lucky," Ricardo said.

"And maybe you are just being deliberately stupid," Melanie snapped back at him. "Why won't you accept that he can be a very dangerous person, and you don't want to get into a pissing contest with him?"

Ricardo shrugged. "I'm not exactly Little Bo-Peep."

+++

Susanne went back to her desk. She tried to get on with some work, but every time she began to do something, she became distracted by thoughts of Val. She kept telling herself to get on with what she was supposed to be doing, but it was no good. She just couldn't seem to focus. She had always thought of herself as a level-headed, sensible person not given to making snap decisions, but she might have to rethink that because, from the moment she had seen Val, she had known that she liked him. Before that day, she had always scoffed at the idea of love at first sight. But that had changed now. Still, no matter what she did, her thoughts were back on Val instead of on what she should be doing. She couldn't stop thinking about him. This was crazy! She had to get on with some work. Melanie had known him for a long time—that was obvious. So, she decided the best thing to do was to ask Melanie about him later. They had talked about when he had been there before, but when was that? She hoped Val and Melanie hadn't been involved. She thought she'd very much like to get to know Mr. Val Frankland a lot better. She thought Val was a very strange name for a man, but maybe not. She knew a guy called Tracie, so why not Val? But that didn't matter. What did matter was that he was there, and she would like to get to know him? Just then Benny spoke beside her making her jump.

"Sorry," Benny said. "I didn't mean to startle you."

"You shouldn't sneak up on people like that," she said.

"I didn't sneak up on you. You were miles away."

"Yeah, sorry. I guess I was. What did you say?"

"I asked what you thought of him?"

"Him who?"

"You know—Val, Melanie's friend."

"He seems nice enough, but we've only just met him, so it's hard to say."

"I don't think I've ever seen Melanie so excited before," Benny said.

"No, I don't think I have either," Susanne agreed. "I'll tell you what—he doesn't look like the kind of guy who could do all those things she said he could do."

"I know what you mean. He looks more like he might want to look at your tax returns," Benny said.

"He could look at my tax returns anytime he wanted," Susanne said.

"Pardon?" Benny asked.

"Sorry," she said. "I guess I was thinking out loud." She could feel herself blushing—her face felt red hot.

"Yeah, I guess you were," Benny said, laughing.

CHAPTER 2

And Introducing ...

Melanie had returned to her lab when Thomes told them to get on with some work, but now she came back. They all looked up at her.

"Don't worry. I have a good reason to be here," Melanie said.

"I hope so," Ricardo said. "Thomes was pretty pissed when he left."

"Well, he won't be when he gets back. I've got some good news for him," she said. "I have those test results he wanted."

"So, come on, tell us who Val is!" Susanne said.

"Oh, he's just an old friend," Melanie replied.

"Are you—were you—and he … you know … together?"

"Good god, no," she said, laughing. "He's like my big brother."

Susanne looked at her questioningly. "Big brother?"

Melanie just smiled and nodded.

"Well, if he's your big brother, I think you have a very cute big brother. Did he work here before? Is that how everybody seems to know him?"

"Yes, he did. He was Thomes's second in command. He did what Ricardo does now."

"Both you and Thomes called him Val. Is that his real name?"

"Yes, he is called Val," Melanie said.

"Val! That's a girl's name." Laughed Ricardo, who had come up behind Susanne. "I knew there was something odd about him."

"Oh, just be quiet," Melanie said.

"Is Val his real name?" Susanne asked.

"Yes, it is," Melanie said. "It's short for Valentine."

"But who is he?" Susanne demanded "I mean, if anyone asks about him, Thomes says be quiet, don't ask. What's the big secret? You said he was here before. What did he do that was so bad? And does he live around here? What does he do? And how can I get his number?"

Melanie burst out laughing. "Sounds like you've got it bad."

"Got what bad?" Susanne said. But she was smiling.

"Well, I don't know where he's living now. As for what he does and whom he works for it looks as though he might be working here."

"I wonder where he comes from?" Ricardo asked. "His accent sounds strange to me. Could be British I suppose."

"What's wrong with you?" Melanie asked. "Are you feeling a bit jealous? Or maybe a bit threatened by him?"

"Why would I feel threatened by him? No, I was just wondering why he's here. I mean why would the boss want him here?"

"If you are referring to Special Agent Thomes and our visitor?" a voice said from behind them. "I don't think that Special Agent Thomes would have wanted him here, not after the last time."

They all turned to see Doctor "Doc" Donald Sibbald, a man of medium height with broad shoulders and a mass of long black hair just starting so show flecks of grey. He wore round John Lennon glasses that were usually resting on the tip of his nose.

"Why what happened last time?" Benny asked.

"You would have to ask Thomes about the details of that," Doc said. "But I'm pretty sure that Val is the last person Thomes would have wanted here. Unless it was to shoot him. Actually, at one point, that is something I thought might be a real possibility." He turned to Melanie. "So, it's true then? He's back."

"Oh, yes. He's back all right. Do you have any idea what's going on?" Melanie asked.

"No, I don't. But whatever it is it can't be good. Not if it involves Val being brought back. I'm willing to bet that the decision to bring him back did not come from Thomes—or the director for that matter. I would be willing to bet my pension that the decision came from much higher up and was passed down for Trena to deal with because I can't see her wanting him back either."

"But who is he?" Benny asked.

Doc put his hand on Benny's shoulder. "My boy, he is one of those strange breeds of people that don't exist. But the fact that he is here probably means that the proverbial something is about to hit the fan."

"Or maybe it already has," Melanie said.

"Could be," Ricardo said. "Just because we haven't heard about anything going down doesn't mean that nothing is."

There was more talk between them about why Val might be there.

"We may never know the why," Doc said. "As a rule, whatever Val is involved in is usually kept under wraps."

"What do you mean by that?" Ricardo asked.

"What I mean is, it's not a very good idea to ask too many questions about him or what he is doing. That kind of thing can be hazardous to your career."

"The CIA doesn't operate on home soil," Benny said.

"Well that's what they tell us," Ricardo said.

"There's one thing I can tell you for certain about Val," Doc said.

"And what is that?" Ricardo asked.

"He doesn't work for the CIA."

"And you know this for certain?" Ricardo said.

"Yes," Doc said. "I do know that for certain."

"How do you know that?" Ricardo asked. "And if he doesn't work for them, it must be one of the other three-letter agencies."

Doc didn't answer. He just shrugged his shoulders. "That is something you will have to ask him about yourself. But I think you'll find that he has the same boss you do."

"How can that be? I've never heard of him before. I still think he works for one of those three-letter agencies. If he still worked for Thomes and the director, I'm sure we would have heard about him. We would probably have heard what he's here for and what he's doing here!" Ricardo said.

Doc gave him a wry smile. "I suppose you could always ask him. But I don't think for one minute he would tell you anything."

"Yeah, that's pretty much what I thought," Ricardo said.

+++

Thomes had taken a seat in the director's office. It was a large, well-appointed room with paneled walls and a large desk. Director Trena Kennedy was a small, delicate-looking woman with mousey brown hair. She looked lost sitting behind the huge desk—like a child playing in her daddy's office. But she was every bit as deadly as the men with whom she had to deal.

Val entered the office a few moments later, he looked first at Thomes and then at the director. And he smiled. "Looks like the gang's all here," he said.

"Yes, the gang's all here as you so eloquently put it. How have you been? asked the director.

"I've been good. But you know that, don't you? You've been keeping track of me, haven't you?"

It was Trena's turn to smile. "Yes, I have. I have to make sure that one of my favorite people is looked after, mustn't I? I'm sure you remember how close we were, don't you?"

Val remembered just how close they had been. They had been lovers for a while, but it hadn't worked out. Val thought that maybe Trena still had feelings for him. "Yes, I remember," Val said.

"Would you remind me why the hell I had him brought back here?" Thomes said, pointing at Val.

"Excuse me, but I can hear you," Val said. "You're talking about me as if I was somewhere else."

"You agreed that we needed to call him back for this job," said the director.

"Yes, I know, but now that he's here … well, I don't know."

"Hello! Did I suddenly become invisible?" Val said.

"Look, for now just add him to your team as a trainee agent, a specialist, or whatever the hell you like. Just sit him at a desk and keep him busy for now. Okay?" Trena said.

"Hello! Can you hear me?" Val said.

Thomes turned to Val. "Well, it looks like I'm stuck with you."

"Oh, so you finally noticed that I'm here," Val said. "After all, you sent for me, didn't you?"

"Yes, I did. And now you're here, and I'm stuck with you. But you're part of the team again. None of this solo lone ranger shit like last time. Is that clear?"

"Yes, sir, as clear as can be. But if you think for one minute that I'm going to be like a dog that you can kick whenever you get upset, you can forget it.

"Right," said the director. "That's enough from both of you. Now, Val, you have been called back to deal with an old adversary of yours."

"And which adversary is that?"

"It's someone who is of concern to all the agencies. They have been trying to get this guy for years, but they have never been able to get anything to stick. Every time anyone gets close, witnesses die, and evidence disappears. A lot of our people have died trying to get this bastard. He always seems to be one step ahead, and he just walks away. So, it has been proposed that the problem should be solved—permanently—while he is here in Washington. And that is where you come in, Val."

"So that's it," Thomes said turning to face Val. "That's what this is all about. That's why I was talked to calling you back. It's about you being a killer. I was talked into sending for you to remove a problem, and just as I should have expected, they send you to kill whoever is creating the problem."

"So, what do you suggest we should do?" Val snapped back at him. "Should we just slap his wrists and say, 'Please don't do that'?"

"You've got an answer for everything, haven't you?"

"No, I don't. And I don't kill for fun. I kill only when I have to when there is no other choice. When I kill, it has been sanctioned. We can't let smug bastards like whoever this is get away with killing people just because he feels like it, or because he gets upset."

"What makes you so different?"

"I've just told you—he kills for fun. I don't."

"I see. It seems to me that you were running around Europe making yourself judge, jury, and executioner. You were killing people at will until you were recalled back home. So, who was telling you then whom to kill and who not to kill? How were you so different then?"

"You seem very well informed about what I was doing while I was in Europe," Val said.

"I don't just take things I'm told as gospel. I check things out for myself. And, let's face it, all I had to do was follow the trail of dead bodies straight to you."

Val knew that Thomes was just trying to get under his skin, trying to make him mad enough to lose control, so he decided to say nothing.

"So, does this smug bastard have a name?" Thomes asked Trena.

"Yes, he does," the director said. "His name is Royce Lyme."

"I'm sure I've heard that name before," Thomes said.

"I'm sure you have. But you might know him better as Luciano."

"Luciano!" Val almost shouted. "Where is he?"

"We don't know exactly where he is, but we know that he's somewhere here in Washington."

"We've never actually met face to face, but I know that low-life scumbag very well," Val said. "At least as well as he knows me, I guess. So, do we know what he's up to here in Washington?"

"We think he's here recruiting people and buying weapons," said Trena. "And that is the reason you're here. A decision is being made as to whether or not you should deal with him on American soil."

Thomes burst out laughing.

"And just what is so funny?" Val snapped at him.

"You," Thomes said, still laughing. "The great Val Frankland brought down to the level of the common man."

"What the fuck are you talking about?" Val said, still sounding angry. "I was dragged back here for a job that someone here could have easily dealt with, and that is if it even happens at all. And I don't get this, if it must be done, I could have done it in Europe."

"I heard you tried that twice before," Thomes said.

"As it happens, I did almost have him twice, once in Paris and again in New York. But I just missed him both times."

"So that's it. At last, the dust begins to settle. Did you request this assignment?" asked Thomes.

"Just what the hell do you mean? And why the hell would I ask to come back here? This is the last place I would ask to be. And it was you who sent for me, remember?"

"Maybe you still think it was Luciano who had a hand in Juliet's death, and that maybe he was behind the attempt on you that cost Juliet number two her life and the bomb in your car that killed Gary. Maybe this is a chance for a little payback."

Val stood and turned sharply to Thomes. He was angry. "Just you leave them out of this. They have nothing to do with this! God damn it! Besides, that had nothing to do with Luciano. It was Archie Waters. Remember—I shot his brother dead, so he tried to kill me, you know that."

"Yes, I remember. But still, Luciano could have been behind it."

Val thought that Thomes hadn't lost his touch. He had tried his best not to let Thomes get under his skin, but he had failed miserably.

"That is enough from both of you," Trena said sharply. "We will have to wait for the final decision. Then we'll see what has to be done and take it from there, okay?"

"Yes," they both said together.

"Good. Then get back to work," she said.

As they made their way back to the squad room, Thomes said, "I want you to keep your contact with the other team members to a minimum. Do you understand?"

"You don't have to worry about that," Val replied. "The sooner I get out of here, the happier I will be."

"Amen to that," Thomes said.

When they got back to the squad room, Ricardo spoke to Thomes. "Doc asked if you would go see him when you got back. He has some information for you. And Melanie said she had the results you've been waiting for."

"Okay. Thank you." He turned to address all the agents. "Now, I know you have all met briefly, so I'll keep this short and sweet. This is Val Frankland. He's going to be joining our team for a while. He's the best at finding people who don't want to be found, and he's here to deal with a domestic issue that has cropped up. We have been having trouble with a certain person who always seems to walk away as free as a bird from any form of prosecution, so we are to give Val any help he might need. Is that understood?"

"Yes," they all said together.

"Right then," Thomes said to Val, "Introductions. This is Ricardo Belin, my senior agent, and undercover specialist. He does all his best work undercover. At least that is what he tells us. And this young woman is Susanne Wilder. She is an artist—the best sketch artist I have ever known. Her ability to get the best out of people is unparalleled. And this young man is Benny Ferral, our technical wizard. He is a wizard with anything electronic. He is the best in the business with computers, phones, any form of communication device or storage device. He can recover any hard drive, and perhaps I shouldn't say this, but he can hack almost anything."

They all said hi, and Val shook hands all round.

"Right then," Thomes said. "Now we all know each other. Val, you're with me. The rest of you get on with some work."

+++

After Thomes and Val had left the squad room, Ricardo sat at his desk brooding. Why was Thomes bringing that asshole into the team? Why did they need him?

"What's wrong with you?" Susanne asked him. "You don't seem very happy about us having a new team member."

"I don't see why we need another team member," Ricardo said. "We are okay with the team we have. I mean just what is he here for? Why do we have to help him? Help him with what? We don't need the likes of him."

"What's wrong? Feeling threatened, are you?" she asked.

"Not at all. Why would I feel threatened by him?"

"You tell me," Susanne said. "It's you who's behaving like a spoiled kid having to share his favorite toy. And, as for why Val is here, why don't you tell Thomes you want to know exactly why Val is here when he gets back?"

"Very funny," Ricardo said. "And for the record, I'm not acting like a spoiled child."

"If you say so. But maybe you should just take it easy. You know, chill out. Thomes will tell us what he wants us to know when he's ready. You know that."

Ricardo said nothing as he went back to his desk, but inside he was furious. The look on his face was a mixture of anger and frustration.

After a while, Ricardo took a break from his desk to use the bathroom and get coffee. While he was away from his desk, he went to the area where the assault course was located. He had heard Melanie ask Val if he was going to run the course while he was there. Val had said that he didn't know, but he might. It must have been a long time since Val had last run the course. But if he decided that he did want to run the course, Ricardo wanted to be ready. The course was laid out like an urban neighborhood with house and shop fronts made from plywood. During a "run", various figures would pop up in the setting. Some of them were bad guys and some were women, children and old folks, and some were what Val called the handsome hubbies. Agents were awarded points for shooting the bad guys, and they lost points for hitting civilians. All of the figures had sensors attached to them to record hits from the special guns they used Ricardo spoke to one of the technicians responsible for the running and maintenance of the course. He asked about how things worked, about all the different settings and what they did. The technician explained it all to him and asked if it was true that Val Frankland was back.

"Do you know him?" Ricardo asked.

"Well, no," the technician said. "But I've heard about him. All of us here at the course have. He's a bit of a legend around here, and as far as I know, he has the best record at the course. Before it was altered, he used to call it the insult course—or so I've been told—because he said it was so easy to complete. So, he helped to toughen it up to what it is today. Now we have a variety of settings from beginner to expert and live fire."

"Live fire? I've never heard of that one."

"I've never seen that one used, but it's there. I've heard that's the setting that Val Frankland used. Again, I don't know for sure, but it could be true, from what I've heard."

"What's your name?" Ricardo asked him.

"My name's Phil," the technician replied.

"Well, Phil, it looks like you have your hands full running all this and remembering who has what setting."

"No, not really," Phil said.

"I could never remember all that," Ricardo said.

"Oh, I'm sure you could. Do you think Mr. Frankland might run the course while he's here? And if he does, do you think I might be able to observe?"

"I think that might be arranged," Ricardo said. "I can't promise anything."

Phil seemed very excited about the prospect and was eager to give Ricardo the full low-down on how the system worked. Ricardo was not nearly in the same league as Benny with this kind of thing, but he was no slouch either. He thought if he got the chance he could rig the course so that mister high and mighty Val Frankland would have to face live rounds instead of laser hits from the guns.

CHAPTER 3

Val and Thomes

When Thomes and Val got to Doc's lab, he was just finishing up with a body on the table. He looked up and saw Val with Thomes.

"So, the rumors are true," he said. "The prodigal has returned. Should we now kill the fatted calf and prepare a feast in your honor?"

"How are you, Doc?" said Val. "I must say, you're looking well."

"Oh, I'm not bad. You know how it is. We have to keep going."

"Yes, we do," Val said. "We most certainly do."

"Well, I must say I'm surprised by your presence. I never thought I would see you here again."

"That makes two of us. But you know what they say about bad pennies—we have a habit of turning up when you least expect us."

"Ricardo said you wanted to see me," Thomes said. "That is if you two have finished."

"Sorry, yes," Doc said. "I have a cause of death on our friend here."

Val tuned them out. He had no interest in what they were saying. He was thinking about when he had been there before. Things were different then. The team was different. It had consisted of himself, Trena, Juliet, and Gary. Thomes had led the team, and of course, Doc and Melanie had supported them. It had been a good team—no, a great team. Then Juliet and Gary had been killed, and that was when things had changed. Thomes had always blamed Val for what had happened to both Juliet and Gary. And maybe he even blamed him for what had happened to Juliet, his late wife, as well. Two Juliet's—each so different, and both so beautiful. Maybe he was to blame. Maybe if he had stayed away from them, they would both be alive today.

Val suddenly realized that Thomes was talking to him. "Sorry," he said "What were you saying? I was miles away."

"Yes, you were. I was asking if you're ready to go back."

"Sorry. Yeah, of course. See you later, Doc."

Doc said goodbye to them, and they left him to get on with his work.

"So, have you thought about this Luciano character and what we're going to do?" asked Thomes.

"You don't need to worry about it. You and your team won't have to be involved in the job. I always work alone—you know that."

"Ah, yes. The famous Lone Ranger," Thomes said. "But this time you're going to have to play by the rules. You heard what the director said. It's time for you to stop being such an ass and play as part of the team."

"Your team isn't trained for this kind of work, they would just get in my way."

"Still as modest as ever," Thomes said. "But you don't get it, do you? This time you're part of the team, like it or not. So, let's talk about what we're going to do.

Val sighed. "Okay. I suppose you're right. I think you and I should be at the sharp end with the others as support. A lot depends on what the powers that be want. Do they want it to look like an accident? Or do they want to send a message? Or maybe they want it to be dealt with quietly. You know, despite everything, it will be good to work with you again."

Thomes was forced to smile. "Yes, it has been a long time, and I'm forced to agree it will be good to work together again. There is still something I don't understand—why did it have to be you?"

"I don't know," Val said. "It's not like I asked to be called back here. All I was told was to book into my hotel and await further orders. I was surprised as hell when I received the orders to report here to you. I just couldn't believe it. I mean, why would you want me here? The orders said you had a domestic issue that required my attention."

"I thought you were busy in Europe," Thomes said.

"I was," Val said. "And I was happy. But now, thanks to you, I'm here."

"It wasn't my idea to recall you. I know I talked about it with the director, and we thought about other agents, but it was decided that that I should send for you."

"Look on the bright side," Val said, laughing.

"There's a bright side?" Thomes said. "You must know something I don't. Somehow I must have missed it."

"There's always a bright side. When you think about it, I could have been assigned to you long term."

"Yes, I see your point."

They walked back to the squad room in silence; each man lost in his thoughts.

+++

Thomes was thinking about when Val was there before. He had been a member of this team. Thomes had been team leader, Val was a senior agent, and Gary and Jules were his other main agents. They had all worked well together; it had been a good team. He remembered when Miss Juliet Linse had joined them. Val had been quite taken with her. He remembered how he used to tease Val about her. Those had been good times back then; he and Val had been brothers. And then everything had gone wrong.

+++

Val was also thinking about the time he was there before, but it hurt to think about it, so he thought he'd be better leaving it alone, but his mind insisted.

+++

Val had been and still was, very good at his job, and over the years he had made a lot of enemies. When he had worked for Thomes, he had been responsible for putting a lot of people behind bars. He was often likened to a terrier; once he got his teeth into something, he just kept gnawing away at it as if it was a bone. He gnawed until he got to the marrow—the truth of the matter.

No matter what he tried to think of, Val's mind insisted on coming back to the team as it had been before things went bad. He thought about Gary Hendon. Gary had looked up to Val as a friend and mentor. One night they were out for a drink in a local bar. Val was going home with a girl who had picked him up, and he asked Gary to drive his car back to his place for the night. Gary had happily agreed to do it. When Gary turned the key to start the car, it had exploded, killing him instantly.

Then Val thought about Juliet—Jules. Val had asked her out for dinner. They were sitting in the restaurant talking, Jules leaned over the table to kiss Val. Just then a sniper's bullet that had been intended for Val had killed Jules instead.

The response to these killings was instantaneous and intense. Task forces were set up, and thorough investigations were conducted. The investigation team went back through Val's old cases looking for clues. The investigators found that the brother of someone that Val had killed in a shootout thought that Val had murdered his brother, so he had decided to get revenge. He had found everything he needed on the internet—how to build a car bomb. When that failed, he decided to shoot Val, so he followed him to the restaurant where he'd killed Jules instead of Val. When the team finally found the man responsible, he had decided he wasn't going to be taken alive, and he shot it out with the agents. He was killed by a hail of bullets, some of them from Val's gun. After it was over, Val would never talk about it. It was clear from the items recovered from the dead man's home that Val had been the target in both cases. There were photos of Val and newspaper clippings describing how Val had broken up a drug ring and had killed the man's brother in the shootout that had taken place during the attempted arrest of the men involved. Several men had been killed, including agents, police officers, and this man's brother. Val was awarded a commendation for his work in breaking up the drug ring. The price of that was that, because of him, two of his friends had been killed. He decided it would be for the best if he left the team before anyone else died. He heard about a new counterterrorism unit that was being set up, so he applied and was accepted to be a part of the team. It was going to be separated from the unit Val was with. Trena Kennedy would nominally be in charge of it, but it wouldn't be a team as such. The operatives would not exist. Only certain people would know of their existence, they would become ghosts, they would work out in the field alone, relying on their skill, and any contacts they made to stay alive and complete their missions. They would live regimented lives keeping the same routine every day, so they could be contacted in case of emergency They would call into their control to receive mission details, then call again to report the end of a mission—its success or failure. It was in this environment that Val had become what he was now. He was a hunter. He would track the terrorist cells down and neutralize any terrorists he found, with extreme prejudice. He became very good at what he did.

+++

Val had always blamed himself for the deaths of Jules and Gary. He supposed he knew that Thomes, and maybe even Trena had also blamed him. That had helped him make up his mind. He thought it would best for everyone if he got out of Washington, out of the United States as soon as he could. So, once he had been accepted for the job, he began his training. He was looking forward to beginning his work in Europe, finding and dealing with terrorists in his way, he felt happy that had taken this chance to begin his new life. His new brief was to hunt down terrorists and neutralize them by whatever means necessary. This was where Val and Thomes disagreed. Thomes thought Val should stay in the United States and continue to do his job using established methods, using the law to bring the terrorists to justice and let the courts decide their fate. Val believed that Thomes's way was flawed. Teams could spend days, weeks, or even months tracking down the bad guys only to have the courts set them free again with a slap on the wrist. In his new job, he wouldn't have to do all that work just to see the terrorists released by some bleeding-heart do-good assholes who had never had to witness first-hand the pain, and carnage caused by these scumbags. No, now he had a free hand, and he would do things his way. Now he would turn things around. He would use their methods against them. Now he would go after them, make them targets, and do as they did with others, he would make them have to keep looking over their shoulders. He would make them think twice before going out. He would make them want to hide, to keep a low profile. The fact was that he would make them feel afraid and unsure. He would make them feel the terror they made others feel.

CHAPTER 4

Susanne's Decision

On their return from talking to Doc, Val, and Thomes walked into the squad room in silence. Val turned to Thomes to ask, "So which desk would you like me to use?

Thomes didn't answer; he just pointed to a desk. Val looked at him and then at the desk. It had been Juliet's desk. Val just stood in front of it for a moment, and once again all the old memories came flooding back. He looked at the desk, he could see Juliet sitting there smiling up at him. Those damn memories; just when he thought he had them all buried deep down and locked away, they had come back to haunt him. He sensed someone beside him. When he turned, he saw Juliet, his late wife? What? How? He gasped.

Juliet smiled at him. "Are you all right?" she asked.

He shook his head and blinked. It was Susanne. "Sorry," he said. "You were saying something."

"I was just asking if you were okay. You looked … you know, as if you had seen a ghost."

"I thought I had," he said very quietly.

"Pardon?" she said.

"Nothing. It's just been a long, tiring day. It must be the jet lag." He smiled.

"Well, if you're sure."

"Yeah, thanks. I'm good."

"Well, if you need anything—anything at all—just let me know."

"Thanks, I will. There is one thing."

"Oh? And what is that?"

"The thing is, I hate to eat alone, and I don't have anyone to eat dinner with tomorrow evening. So, I was just wondering if maybe you would care to have dinner with me. I understand, of course, that you may have to ask Thomes for permission first."

She looked at him. "I don't need to ask anyone for permission to do anything," she said angrily.

"Sorry. I didn't mean to upset you. It's just that I know Thomes will have told everyone to stay away from me."

"That's okay. But I don't understand why he doesn't want any of us to come near you or to get friendly with you."

Val laughed. "Maybe he thinks I'll be a bad influence on you. He might be worried that I'll lead you astray."

"And will you?"

"Will I what?"

She smiled. "Lead me astray, of course."

"You never know. I just might do that."

"All right," she said. "I think I might risk it. But only if I get to choose the restaurant."

A smile spread across his face. "All right, you get to choose where we eat. But does that mean you'll be choosing the most expensive restaurant you can find?"

"Of course I will. Don't you think I'm worth it?"

"Yes, of course, I think you're worth it. So, I'll let you make the reservations then, shall I?"

"I think maybe I can handle that."

"Good. I'll look forward to it."

Susanne went back to her desk. Ricardo watched her.

"What the hell was all that about?" Ricardo asked. "What the hell do you think you're doing?"

"It's none of your business," she said.

Ricardo turned to Val, who was now sitting at his desk tapping away on his computer keyboard. "So, what should we call you? Should we call you Val or do you prefer Valentine? Or is there another name you might prefer us to use?"

"You can call me whatever you like as long as it's not late for breakfast. I seem to remember that Thomes told you my name. But I have also been known to answer to 'hey, you' and 'hey, handsome'," he said smiling.

"What are you smiling at?" Ricardo asked.

"Nice try, Ricky Boy, but I take it you're not having a lot of luck?"

"I don't know what you're talking about."

"No? Okay then. I'll let you play the game your way."

"What are you two going on about?" Susanne asked.

"Well, Ricky here doesn't like or trust me, and he's been running my name through as many databases as he can. He's trying to find information about me—like who I am, where I come from, what I do. That sort of thing. But so far, he hasn't found anything. Isn't that right, Ricky Boy?"

Ricardo just sat at his desk saying nothing.

"Okay, then. You see, he thinks if he can get more information about me, it might help his search. Isn't that right, Ricky Boy?"

"Don't call me Ricky. My name is Ricardo."

"Yeah, okay. Sorry, Ricky. I'll try to remember that. Now, I'll tell you something that you might find useful. It doesn't matter how many names you try for me; it won't help you one little bit."

"How do you know what he's doing?" Susanne asked. "He might not be searching for you at all."

"Oh, yes, he's searching all right," Val said.

"But how do you know for sure what he's doing?" Susanne asked, sounding puzzled.

"It's easy. All these computers are networked together, right, Benny?"

"Yes, of course," Benny replied.

"So, I have it all on my screen, and I can see exactly what Ricky Boy is doing."

"No, you can't do that," Benny said. "Yes, they are all networked together, but not so you can share information unless someone sends it to you. They're not set up like that."

"Well then, this must be a hallucination on my screen. Come and look for yourself."

Both Benny and Susanne went to Val's desk.

"Well I'll be damned," Benny said. "How did you do that?"

"It's just a little trick I picked up that's all."

"A little trick?" Benny said. "I thought I was supposed to be the technical expert. Just what is it you do?"

"Think of me as a mechanic, or maybe a handyman. In any case, when things get broken, I fix them."

"So, what is it that's broken here?" Benny asked.

Val just smiled. "Nothing that you need to worry about," he said.

"Okay," Ricardo said. "I'll admit that I've been searching, trying to find out who you are. So, what?"

"You don't like me, do you?" Val said.

Ricardo just looked at him saying nothing.

"For what it's worth," Val continued, "your bosses are probably not very happy about this either, but that doesn't matter. The only thing that matters is the job I'm here for. It doesn't matter what the job entails; it could be just to stay attached to this team. So, what you, the director, or Thomes thinks of me doesn't matter."

"So, what is this job you're here for?" Ricardo asked.

"I'm afraid that is need to know. And you don't need to know. You have all the information you need for now. But, like it or not, it could mean me just staying here as a member of this team, for quite some time." Val said. "But whatever it is, it must be something you're not good enough to handle."

Ricardo stood and moved towards Val.

"Sit down before you get hurt," Val said.

"You don't scare me," Ricardo said. He glared at Val but sat down again.

"I wasn't trying to scare you. I was just saving you from getting hurt."

"Okay you can't tell us why you're here, so can you tell us why Thomes and the director hate you so much?"

"Hate is such a strong word," said Val. "But as for why they don't seem to like me, Thomes told you all you need to know about that."

There was a silence between them that was broken by the telephone ringing and making them all jump. Benny answered it. "Yes, right away," he said. "That was the director, Val. She wants you and Thomes to go up to her office now."

"Do you know where Thomes went?" Val asked.

"I think he went to see Melanie," Benny said. "I'll give her a call and ask her to let him know."

"Please do. Oh, and just a word to the wise, Ricky Boy: If you insist on running my name through databases, you might find some rather large guys in black suits asking you a lot of awkward questions about why you want such information, so you might want to think about the fact that doing the things you're doing can be hazardous to your career. If you insist and continue with this pointless search for me, not even Thomes or the director will be able to protect you." With that, he turned and walked out of the room. They all stood and watched him go.

+++

Val left the squad room and walked towards the stairs that led to the director's office. He walked slowly, not looking where he was going. He was thinking about what had just happened. Why was he pushing Ricardo? What did he hope to achieve by doing that? Was he trying to impress Susanne, or did he want Ricardo to push back, to force a confrontation?

"No, that's stupid," he said aloud. But was it? He had been twisting Ricardo's tail since he first walked into the squad room. As he was going through this in his mind, he walked right into Agent Thomes.

"What the hell?" Thomes said, sounding surprised. "What the hell are you doing?"

"Sorry," Val said. "I wasn't watching where I was going."

"Yes, I noticed that. And where are you going?" Thomes asked.

"I'm on my way to the director's office. She sent for me."

"Don't bother. She doesn't want either of us." Thomes said, still looking at Val

"Benny said she called the squad room and told them to send you and me up here," Val said.

"Yes, I know that. But I just spoke to her, and she said it doesn't matter now. Are you sure you're okay?"

"Yes. I'm fine."

"Look, I know things have been a bit bad between us, but I never hated you. You know that, right? So I was thinking that now that you're

37

back, even if it is for a short while; well I thought that maybe we could, you know, sort of patch things up a little. Put the past behind us"

Val looked at him, shock showed on his face. "Are you serious?"

Thomes nodded. "It's been a long time. Maybe too long to hold a grudge. So, what do you say?"

"I say that it sounds like you're getting soft in your old age. But I also think it's a great idea. You're right. It has been too long."

"Don't think you're going to get any special treatment or anything. And for the record, I still think you were wrong to take this job of yours. You were a damn good investigator. You understand people and what made them tick."

"Thank you. But I'm also good at what I do now."

Thomes shook his head. He could feel his anger rising. "You can be such an ass. Okay, let's forget about the job you do now, and just for a while, pretend you're one of the team again."

Val smiled. "Yeah. Sorry, boss."

+++

"I hope this is the job he's here to do," Ricardo said. "Then we can get rid of him; we don't need him here."

"He's right, isn't he?" Susanne asked. "It burns you to think of him getting things he wants."

He looked at her. "You like him, don't you?" he said.

"It's none of your business. Whom I like or dislike has nothing to do with you or anyone else for that matter? But it's obvious that you don't like him."

"You want to be very careful," Ricardo said. "If Thomes finds out that you're going out to dinner with him, he won't be very happy about it. He said we should stay away from him, remember?"

"Yes, I do remember, and just who is going to tell him, you?"

Ricardo held up his hands. "No, not me," he said.

"Whom I go out to dinner with has nothing to do with anyone here."

"I was just saying that Thomes won't be pleased about it, that's all."

"Well, since it's me and not Thomes who is going out with him, I don't see the problem. I can see anyone I want to see when I'm on my own time."

"So, who is going out with whom?" a voice behind them asked.

They both turned to see Melanie. "Come on," she said. "Don't keep me in suspense! Who is going out with whom?"

"Our Susanne here is going out to dinner with him," Ricardo said gesturing with his chin towards the door.

"Him who?" Melanie said. "Do you mean Val?"

"Who else would I mean?"

Melanie turned to Susanne. "That's fantastic news. He asked you out. I wondered if he might."

Susanne turned to Ricardo. "You should learn to keep your nose out of other people's business." She turned back to Melanie. "Yes, he did. I know Thomes said to stay away from him, but I don't see the harm in going to dinner with him. Do you? And what did you mean you thought he might?"

"Oh, it was just the way he looked at you, that's all. I think it's so exciting."

"Can't you tell us anything about him?" Benny asked.

"There is one thing I can tell you."

"Yeah, and what is that?"

"I can tell you that Susanne will have a good time out with Val."

"How long have you known him?" Susanne asked.

"I've known him for a lot of years, but not as long as Thomes, Doc, or the director."

"I can't understand why they all seem to hate him. They just keep saying it was something that happened when he was here last time. What happened that was so bad?"

"You'll have to ask them about that," Melanie said. "But I think saying they hate him is a bit strong."

"What do you mean a bit strong?"

"I know it looks as if they hate Val, but I don't think they do—not really. It's just complicated. Before you start asking more questions, you would be better off asking Thomes or the director. Or you could even try asking Val himself."

"Well, seeing as we're going out to dinner tomorrow evening, I might just do that," Susanne said.

"I wish you the best of luck with it," Melanie said smiling.

Susanne smiled. "You don't think he'll talk to me, do you?" She asked.

+++

Melanie inclined her head toward the door. "Walk with me," She said. Susanne got up from her desk and went with her. They left the squad room and walked towards the area she called her den. It was the laboratory where she worked her forensic magic. "I want to tell you a story about Val. When I first met Val, I was only a teenager when we first met, I thought he was an arrogant son of a bitch, he was always strutting around like he owned the place. Then there came a day when two guys I had gone out on dates with got together. I had gone out only once with each of them, but they got together and decided they were going to take from me what I wouldn't give them willingly. They attacked me; they were waiting for me when I left a restaurant after having a meal with some girlfriends. I had never been so frightened in my life. Luckily for me, Val came along and pulled them off me and, to use his words, he explained things to them. But in plain English, I can tell you that he beat the shit out of them. Then he wrapped his jacket around me to cover where my clothes had been torn, then he took me home. At first, my mother and father thought it was Val who had attacked me, but once I explained that it was Val who had saved me from being raped by two men, my mom and dad couldn't thank him enough. They thought he was the best thing since sliced bread. As far as they were concerned, he walked on water. From then on, he became like a big brother to me. I think Mom and Dad hoped he would be Mr. Right, that Val and I would marry raise a family, and live happily ever after. But it was never like that between us. We became the best of friends, and that is how things have been from that day to this. Back then, he put the word around that anyone who tried anything like that again would end up like those other guys. If anyone said anything to me or even looked at me wrong, they would have to answer to him. He has been there for me ever since. If I ever need him, he's always there for me. All I have to do is call him. I never blamed him for what happened to Gary and Juliet. But I do, however, think that Thomes and the director did. I've heard that he has been married, but his wife died. I don't know what happened, and he wouldn't talk about it. I think that he also blamed himself for Gary and Juliet. And maybe that's why he won't talk about his ex-wife—or what happened to her. He won't talk about Gary or Juliet either. I also think that's part of the reason he left last time. But that doesn't matter, he's back here again."

"So, what happened to this Gary and Juliet? Susanne asked.

Melanie thought for a few moments, then she explained what had happened, how both Gary and Juliet had been killed. How both times it had been Val who was the target.

CHAPTER 5

Val and Susanne

Val was sitting at his desk just looking into space. He was brought out of his thoughts by Thomes, who came and stood in front of his desk. "Can I help you?" Val asked.

"Yes, you can. You said that you know this Luciano and that he knows you. Tell me about Luciano," Thomes said.

"What can I tell you that you don't already know?" Val said.

"I don't mean what's in the files. I mean how it came about that you were chasing him all over the world."

Val thought for a moment then said, "You know that, after training, when I left here, I found an apartment and based myself in Paris?"

"Yes, of course, I know. We had to keep an eye on where the money was going. But what has that got to do with anything?"

"Yes, you kept an eye on me, didn't you?" Val said, smiling.

Benny, Susanne, and Ricardo came and stood behind Thomes to listen to what Val was saying. "Well, I was still finding my way around, getting a feel for my new job. I was sitting in a street café having a coffee when I heard some guys at the next table talking about Luciano. They were huddled together speaking English. I think they thought I couldn't understand. They were talking about terrorist activities—drugs, weapons, and an upcoming attack at Disneyland. I called it in and got permission to take the case on. It was my first case, and I went after them. I got four of the terrorists, but I missed Luciano, and I've been chasing him ever since. I also missed him in New York. He seems to have an uncanny knack for knowing when I get close to him. A few times he's tried to have me killed, but as you can see, so far he hasn't had any luck."

"Shame," Ricardo muttered.

"What did you say?" Thomes asked him.

"I said it's a shame that Val missed him," Ricardo answered.

"Okay, so you know this Luciano, in a manner of speaking, and you say that he knows you," continued Thomes.

"Yeah, so what?"

"Does he know what you look like?"

Val shrugged his shoulders. "I guess he could know what I look like. I've been chasing the son of a bitch for years. I've seen a photo of him, so I would say it's more than likely he would have seen one of me. Why?"

"We need to find him—to find out what he's doing, where he's staying."

Thomes turned to the rest of the team. "Right. I want you out there. Talk to all of your contacts. Call in all favors. I want to know where this guy is and what he's doing. Come on, people. Let's go."

"We don't know what he looks like," Ricardo said.

"So, does everyone you look for send you photos?" Thomes said sarcastically. "Val can describe him to you but use the skills I thought you had. Now move."

"What about me?" Val asked.

"No," Thomes said. "I want you to work with Susanne to sketch this guy. If you're out there looking for him, he might run. Plus, Ricardo, Benny, and Susanne have more contacts here than you do. So, until we get the final decision, I don't want to spook him."

"He probably already knows that I'm here in Washington. He has an excellent information network."

"Yes, maybe he does. But he might not know that you know he's here. So, it will be best if you stay out of sight and just keep the others updated with any information they require. You should keep a low profile for now."

"I don't like the idea of just sitting around doing nothing."

"You won't be sitting around doing anything. You don't have to worry about that. You'll be collating all the information these three are going to collect—aren't you?" Thomes said, looking at Ricardo, Susanne, and Benny."

"Yes, sir," they all chorused together.

"Okay, if you think that's the way to go," Val said.

"I do. Now go with Susanne and get that sketch done."

When Susanne's sketch was finished, Val marveled at it. She was, indeed, a great artist. "You are good at this aren't you?" he said.

"Thank you very much, kind sir," Susanne said, smiling.

Susanne made several copies of her sketch and gave them out to the other members of the team.

Armed with their copies, they went out to talk to as many of their contacts as they could.

+++

When Val arrived the following morning, Thomes and the other team members were already there.

"You're late," Thomes said.

"Sorry, boss," Val said. "I was working late last night. It won't happen again."

"So, what do you have for me?" Thomes asked.

Val handed Thomes a folder. Thomes opened it and read the contents. "Thank you for this. Now please bring the others up to speed, will you? I'll take this and talk to the director." With that Thomes walked off towards the director's office.

The team members all looked at Val.

"The reason I was working late last night was that I was talking to some of my contacts in Europe. It seems that Luciano dropped out of sight about three months ago. No one has seen or heard anything about him, so I checked with immigration, and it seems that my old friend Luciano—or Royce Lyme if you prefer—flew into Boston's Logan Airport about three months ago. Then he disappeared. That's the report I just gave Thomes. He will talk to the director and see if they think they need to alert Homeland Security. Luciano could well be planning something big, so we do need to find him."

Val went to his desk and sat down. He was just staring into space.

Susanne walked over and sat in the chair next to his desk. "Are you all right?" she asked.

"Yeah, I'm fine. I'm just a little tired. Why do you ask?"

"You just looked so sad."

"I was just thinking about Luciano and what he's up to. But I'm fine—honest. Have you made our reservations for this evening?"

She smiled at him. "Yes, I have."

"Good! That means you haven't changed your mind. It gives me something to look forward to."

"Yeah, me too," she said.

"So, are you going to tell me where we're going?"

She giggled. "No," she said. "I want it to be a surprise. I will say that I've always wanted to try this place, but I could never afford it."

Val smiled at her. "Really?"

"Yes." She smiled at him then flipped her hair back and went back to her desk.

The way she flipped her hair and the way she moved reminded him of his late wife. Once again, he asked himself what he was doing, she isn't Juliet he told himself. He shook himself and tried to get on with some work. He couldn't help it; his mind was like a kitten playing with a ball of wool. His mind kept returning to Susanne and what might be happening to him. A little at a time he became wrapped up in his work until his stomach rumbled. *I'm hungry.* He thought and laughed. He had just stood to go out for some lunch when Benny and Susanne returned to the office. Benny held out a sandwich to him. "I was talking to Thomes, I told him we were calling for some sandwiches, I asked him what kind of sandwich you might want," Benny told Val. "We brought you a roast beef and horseradish with red onions. I hope that's okay."

"That's great," Val said. "Who do I owe for the sandwich?"

"It's okay," said Benny. "The boss paid for them."

"It sounds disgusting," Ricardo said.

"Just as well you're not eating it," Val retorted.

Ricardo glared at him but said nothing else.

"Oh, I don't know. It sounds sort of nice," Susanne said.

Ricardo looked at her. He seemed about to say something but then changed his mind.

Thomes came back and saw his team standing in the middle of the room.

"What the hell is this? I'm not paying you to stand around like a gaggle of mothers outside the school gates.

"Sorry, boss," they all said, and they went to their desks.

"Thank you for my sandwich, Dex," Val said with a grin on his face.

"You're welcome. And—"

"Yes, I know—stop calling you that."

Thomes surprised the other members of the team by grinning. They had expected him to blow up at Val. "See? You're getting the idea," Thomes said. He was standing in front of Val's desk.

"Is there something else I can do for you?" Val asked him.

"As it happens, yes there is. I hear you're planning on running the 'insult' course."

Val laughed. "Oh, and just who told you that?"

"I have my sources," Thomes said.

"I'm sure you do. Well, for your information, I have not said that I would run the course. Melanie asked me if had thought about doing it while I was here. She said she wanted to know if I was still as good as I used to be and if I was going to try to break my record."

"So, do you think you might give a try?" Thomes asked.

"I don't know. It wasn't something I was planning on. Why do you ask? Are you challenging me?"

"And if I am? Does that scare you?"

Val laughed. "Hell, no. And if that is a challenge, then I accept. I was just beginning to think it would be boring here. So, when do you want to do it?"

"I'll speak to Trena. If she clears it, I'll make the arrangements," Thomes said. And with that, he went back to his office.

"Wow," Benny said. "Are you going to challenge Thomes on the assault course?"

"If the director clears it, yes."

"Do you think you'll beat him?" Susanne asked him.

"Now, that is a good question. Beating him is in no way a sure thing! But please don't tell him I said that. He might get a swelled head." The others laughed at that.

They had all settled down to get back to work when Thomes came back into the room with Director Kennedy, and they approached Val's desk. Val had just finished eating his sandwich. Susanne, Benny, and Ricardo looked up from what they were doing to watch what going to happen.

"Thomes, Director," Val said. "Is there something I can do for you?"

"Maybe there is," Trena said. "Thomes here tells me that you're willing to take him on at the assault course."

"You know me. I'm not one to refuse a challenge."

"Okay, then, what about going around now?"

"Why not?" Val said. "I could do with a break from all this paperwork Thomes has me doing."

"All right then. Let's do it," Trena said. "Thomes, Val, you're with me. The rest of you make your way to the observation area."

"Who goes first?" Benny asked.

"Why?" Trena asked. "What difference does it make?"

"No difference," Benny said, blushing for no apparent reason. "I was just wondering that's all."

"Maybe I should go first," Val said. "Give the old man a target to aim for."

"I'll give you old man," Thomes said. "First or last, it doesn't matter. This old man is still going to kick your ass."

Val laughed. "We'll see about that."

+++

Val and the director followed Thomes to the beginning of the course, Ricardo, Benny, and Susanne had made their way to the viewing area. Thomes spoke to the control room, told them what he wanted. Then he entered the course, and the door closed and locked behind him. He picked up the pistol they used when going around the course. Thomes moved forward, he looked quickly at the array of house and shop fronts that made up the plywood urban center, scoping out areas where figures might pop up. He held the pistol that fired laser beams and began to go through the course, shooting the armed men and women targets and sparing the "innocents." When he had completed the course, his score was calculated. He had scored ninety-five percent.

"There you go," Thomes said to Val when he exited the course. "Let's see you beat that!"

Susanne watched with interest as Val got ready and then entered the course. The door closed and locked behind him. As Val picked up the laser pistol, a klaxon sounded, and red lights began to flash. Susanne's heart leaped into her mouth—something was wrong.

"What the hell is going on?" Thomes bellowed. He picked up the phone to talk to the control room. "What the hell are you playing at?" he shouted at the operator. "This was supposed to set to expert, not *live fire.*"

"I know," the operator said. "But it changed when Agent Frankland entered the course, and it's stuck in this setting! I can't get it to change. It looks like he'll have to go around with it as it is."

"The hell he will! Put me through to speak to him."

"Okay," the operator said. "You're through. Go ahead."

"Val, this is Thomes. Something has gone wrong. The setting is stuck on live fire, and we can't alter it or open the door at the moment, so just stay put until we fix it."

"Don't worry about it. Watch and learn, old man. Watch and learn." Val removed his jacket. He carried two guns—one on his hip and the other in a shoulder holster. He unholstered both.

"No! Don't be stupid," Thomes shouted. "Wait!" But it was too late. Val had started moving.

As they watched, Val went through the course. As he made his way through the course, every one of his shots was on target. He never even came close to hitting a civilian. The main difference here was that, instead of laser beams, the test site was firing live rounds back at him.

Susanne had her heart in her mouth several times thinking he'd been hit, but he kept moving. "It's amazing … absolutely amazing," she said.

Val got through the course and stood to face the final enemy— the archer. It fired three arrows at him. He caught the first one and deflected the second two. Once that was done, the exit door opened. They all went to meet him.

"Are you, all right?" Susanne asked. "Oh, my God, you've been hit! You're bleeding!"

"It's nothing," he said. "I just got grazed by a ricochet. Apart from that, I'm fine. But what the hell happened?"

"I don't know," Thomes said. "But I intend to find out. Ricardo, I want you to start an investigation into what the hell is happening. Use whomever you need, but not Benny or Susanne. I want them to stay on Luciano. You should start with the course operator. Take the console apart if you have to. I want to know just what the hell happened in there."

"Okay, boss. I'm on it."

+++

Ricardo made his way to the assault course control room. The engineer, Phil, whom Ricardo had spoken to before, was still there looking extremely morose. "This is nothing to worry about," Ricardo told him, "but I need to talk to you about what happened when Agent Frankland entered the course."

"I—I don't know what happened," Phil stammered. "Everything was fine when Agent Thomes went through, and then when Agent Frankland entered the course, I pressed the button to start the course and everything just seemed to change on its own! I couldn't do anything about it. I couldn't change it or turn it off—honest."

Was there anyone else here?" Ricardo asked. "Another technician? Or maybe a cleaner?"

"No, I'm the only one here today. I really am sorry. I can't understand it."

"Have you touched anything since Agent Frankland ran the course?"

"No, sir. I left everything just it as it was."

"Good. I'll look at it in a moment. Now I want you to get everyone else who works on the course here. I need to speak to them."

Phil looked puzzled. "Why do you need the others, they weren't here."

"Yes, I know that, but I still want to talk to them, Okay?" Ricardo said.

"Yes, sir. I'll call them all now."

Phil went to an adjacent office to make the calls to bring everyone in. While Phil was doing that, Ricardo stayed in the control room. He used the time to put things back to normal and removed the evidence of what he had done before anyone else could find it. He had rigged the system so that whoever went second would face a live-fire situation. If Thomes had gone second, it wouldn't have mattered because he wouldn't have run the course until it was fixed, so it was a win-win situation. He also knew that Val wouldn't back down from the challenge.

When the rest of the crew who ran the assault course arrived, Ricardo interviewed them all one at a time, but of course, none of them could shed any light on what had happened. Then he had them check over the console to see if they could find anything wrong. But, of course, they found nothing.

When Ricardo returned to the office and reported that he hadn't found anything, he said to Thomes, "I've interviewed all the staff on the course, I can't find anything to suggest any of them had done anything to sabotage the course. But I've told them that I want an engineer to look at this see if he can find anything. I've said he should take the damn thing apart if necessary, I also told the technicians to tell the engineer to disable the live-fire function until further notice. It seems that someone here wants Val dead, and I want to know who that someone is."

"I didn't think you cared," Val said.

"It's not a case of me caring. I just want to tell whoever it is to get in line," Ricardo said.

"Val," said Thomes, "you get yourself down to see Doc and then go home. I don't want to see you again until tomorrow."

"I'm all right," Val said. "No harm no foul."

"It wasn't a request," Thomes said.

Val looked at him for a moment. "Okay. You're the boss." He turned to leave. "I'll see you this evening," he said quietly to Susanne as he walked past her.

Susanne nodded at him.

+++

Val walked into Doc's surgery. "Well, look who's here!" Doc exclaimed. "And what can I do for you?"

Val held up his arm. "Thomes said I should come and see you about this."

"Come on, then. Get your shirt off and let's see what you've done."

Val removed his shirt, and Doc looked at his arm. "So, what have you been up to?"

"It's nothing. Just a graze from going around the course."

"What! Are you saying that Trena let you go around with the live fire setting?"

"No way," Val said, laughing. "No, there would have been too much paperwork if something had gone wrong."

"Looks like things did go a little wrong."

"Only a little."

"Come on, then, let's get a dressing on that." Doc looked him over, noticing multiple scars. "Looks as if a few things have gone a bit wrong."

"Yeah, it seems that not everybody likes me."

"It sure looks that way. Have you thought it might be time to hang it up?"

"Every day, Dad, every day."

Doc smiled. "It's been a long time since you called me that."

"Yeah, I know. But then it's been a long time since I was here."

"That's true. Do you mind if I ask you something?"

"Ask away."

"Well, we have heard things back here, tales of…shall we say— your exploits have trickled back? And now, after looking at your body, I have to ask: are you trying to get yourself killed?"

Val straightened, "What the hell are you talking about? Why would you think that?"

"It's like I said—seeing the scars on your body and hearing about how you rush into things …blindly."

"Well for your information—and for everyone else who thinks the same." Val said, raising his voice just a bit, "the answer is no, I am not trying to get myself killed."

"Okay. No need to shout."

Doc finished cleaning the graze on Val's arm and applying a dressing. "That's it. You're all done. And I'm sorry if I upset you. It's just that I care about you, and I worry. That's all."

"Yeah, I know," Val said. "I didn't mean to shout. I was just shocked. I mean why the hell would you think such a thing."

Doc shrugged but said nothing. Val left Doc and made his way back to his hotel to get ready for his dinner date with Susanne. He thought about what Doc had asked: "Are you trying to get yourself killed?" Was he trying to get himself killed? No. The idea was ridiculous, wasn't it? Of course, it was. The idea was prosperous.

Val called a cab and arrived at Susanne's home at seven as they had arranged. "Hi," he said as she opened her door.

"Hi back," she said. "Are you sure you're all right?"

Val looked puzzled. "All right?" he said.

"You know—from where that bullet hit you."

Val laughed. "I'm fine. It's like I said—it was nothing. It did make a hole in my shirt sleeve though. Do you think I should put in a claim for a new one? I went to see Doc as ordered. He cleaned it and put a band-aid on it, fixed me up like new. So, can we go for dinner now? I'm starving."

"Okay, if you're sure."

"I am. Now, where are we going?"

She smiled a little nervously. "I booked us a table at Cityzen. It's on Maryland Avenue. I hope that's okay."

He took her hand and kissed it. "Of course it is."

"I was a bit worried because it is a bit expensive. I've always fancied eating there, but as I said, I couldn't afford it."

He kissed her hand again. "It's fine, honest. Come on. Let's go."

During their dinner, Susanne asked him how he knew the director, Thomes, and Doc.

"I've known them for a lot of years. I know you've heard people say 'When he was here before …'"

Her smile lit up her face. "Just once or twice," she said.

"I have known Trena and Thomes since I was a kid, but Doc? Well, that's a story for another time."

"Is it that bad?" Susanne asked quizzically.

Val smiled at her. "No, it's just long and drawn out—a story for a rainy night sitting in front of a fire with a bottle of wine when there's nothing on TV."

"Okay then. I'll wait for a rainy night and ask you again." They laughed together.

After dinner, Val took her for drinks, and then they went dancing. Susanne noticed the looks he was getting from other women. She could imagine them wishing it was them with Val. A few of the women did try to talk to Val. He was very polite but kept his attention on Susanne, which made her very happy. She thought that this must be the best date she had ever been on, and she found herself wishing that it would never end.

+++

Susanne arrived at the office early, as was normal for her. But she couldn't remember a thing about the drive to work, and she didn't think her feet had touched the floor from the parking garage. Melanie, Benny, and Ricardo were already there waiting for her.

"By the look of you, I would hazard a guess that your date went well," said Melanie. "So, come on, tell."

"Yeah, come tell us," Benny said.

She looked at them all. "It was magic," she said. "I don't know how to put it into words."

"Try," Melanie said.

"Well, we went for dinner at Cityzen."

"Wow, he took you there?" Melanie said.

"He must earn a lot more than we do," Ricardo said. "Or he put it on expenses."

"You always have to try to spoil things, don't you," Melanie said. "Go on, Susanne, tell us the rest."

"It was fantastic. After dinner, we had a few drinks and went dancing. He's a great dancer."

"Yeah, I know," Melanie said. "You should see all the medals and cups he has for it."

Just then Val walked in. Ignoring everyone, he just walked to his desk and sat down. The others looked at him and then at each other.

There was silence in the room. It was Val who eventually broke the silence. "Is Thomes in yet?" he asked.

"No," Benny said. "But he should be here soon."

"Good. When he gets here, please tell him I'm on my way to the director's office. If she's in?"

"We don't know if she's here or not," Benny said. "She's usually here by now, and so is Thomes."

"Okay. Not to worry. But please tell Thomes where I've gone."

Val got to the door, he had just put his hand on the handle when Melanie called to him, "Is this about this domestic issue that Thomes told us about, and that we're supposed to help you with?"

He didn't answer straight away, he just smiled. "I'll talk to you later, but it's Ralph, okay?"

"Ralph? Really? You mean it?"

He shrugged and nodded. "Yeah, I think so."

"Oh, my god, that is such good news," she said.

"What the hell are you two talking?" Ricardo asked.

"Melanie knows what I'm talking about," said Val. "Thomes will know as well."

He turned and walked away in the direction of the director's office. They all stood and watched him go. They looked at each other. Melanie looked at Susanne had tears in her eyes. "I don't understand," she said. "We had such a wonderful time last night, and then this morning he didn't even look at me. What have I done?"

"I don't know," Melanie said. "I don't think you've done anything wrong, and if it's Ralph?"— Melanie shrugged. "I just don't know."

+++

Val walked along the corridor, lost in his thoughts. What the hell was he doing? Susanne was a nice girl, but she wasn't Juliet. Had he thought that being with her was going to be just like having Juliet back? Susanne looked quite a lot like her, and she had many of Juliet's mannerisms. But she wasn't Juliet, but damn it, he was attracted to her he couldn't help it. What the hell was he going to do? He stopped suddenly he realized there was only one thing he could do, the answer was right in front of him; there was only one thing he could do.

+++

"What does that mean?" Susanne asked. "What does Ralph mean?"

Melanie smiled. "I think it would be best if you were to ask him about that yourself," said Melanie. "Or maybe you could even ask Thomes."

"What the hell are you so happy about?" Ricardo asked Melanie. "Why won't anyone give a straight answer about this guy? And what is it with this Ralph? Does it mean the job he's here for is going to happen?"

"I don't know about that," Melanie said.

"Once he does this job—whatever it is—he'll be gone again, won't he?" asked Susanne.

"I suppose he might," Melanie said. Susanne looked sad. "But he might not be. If it's Ralph … well, we will just have to wait and see."

Just then Thomes arrived and asked where Val was.

"He said he was going to see the director's, and that we should tell you it's Ralph," Melanie said.

"It's Ralph my ass," Thomes said.

"What does that mean?" Susanne asked. "What is Ralph?"

"It means nothing," Thomes said. "Now why is everyone standing around like it's a holiday? Get to work."

+++

Thomes turned and headed for the director's office. When he got there, Val was already there seated in the director's office.

"All right let's get down to it," said Thomes. "What the hell is this about?"

"Is there any chance that yesterday was just an accident? You know, a fault in the machine?" Trena asked.

"I suppose it's possible," said Thomes, "but I don't think it was. Until we know any difference, we are treating this as foul play until we know for certain, one way or the other. I have Ricardo investigating. I'm sure he'll get to the bottom of what's going on. I hate the thought of it being one of us, but it must be. I suppose that Benny knows, but he was with us all the time. The only person who left us was Ricardo, but he doesn't have the skill. I can't see it being the operator. He would have known that he would automatically be a suspect, besides he just wanted to see Val complete the course not watch him get killed."

Thomes stopped talking. He looked at Val then the director. "Okay, so I guess the reason we're isn't to do with what happened at the assault course. Is it? So, tell me what's going on?"

Trena smiled. "You're right this isn't about what happened at the course. It seems we have a bigger problem than a possible glitch in the assault course software, or someone trying to kill Val if that is what happened," said the director.

Thomes looked at her. "And what problem is that?"

"A twelve-year-old girl called Sara Lever has gone missing. It seems that she has been abducted."

"A missing person is a job for the local police," said Thomes. "Or the FBI if it's a kidnapping.

"Yes, under normal circumstances that would be so," said the director, "but these circumstances are not normal. You see, Sara Lever happens to be the daughter of one of our own. Her mother, Laura, works in the finance department. She's responsible for the movement of large amounts of money all over the world, so if she were to send a few million to a different account no one would question it, at least not immediately. The kidnappers have been in touch to say they have Sara."

"What happened?" Thomes asked.

"Mom was at work and Dad was looking after the little girl. They were just getting ready to go out to do some shopping when the kidnappers barged their way into the house. They shot the dad. Fortunately, he's still alive. He's at the hospital in a serious but stable condition. They grabbed Sara and contacted Laura to say they had her daughter and that she should go home and wait for them to get in touch with her to give her their demands. They told her that, if she went to the police, her daughter would die. So, she came to us for help instead."

"Do we have anything to go on?" Thomes asked.

"They called her to let her speak to Sara. We got a partial trace, so we have an area, but when they call back, I want Benny to trace the call."

"So why is Val here?" asked Thomes. "Is he coming in with us?"

"No," Trena said. "He's not going in with you, when we find them, he's going in instead of you."

"Instead of— You have got to be joking," Thomes said.

"No, this is no joke. It has been decided that he is best qualified for this job, so Val goes in alone to get the girl. I'll leave you to work out the details with your team."

"What about you?" Thomes said, turning to Val. "You haven't said a word. What's wrong?"

"Nothing is wrong," Val answered. "I've already told the director what I think about this."

"And what do you think about this?"

"I think it's like using a sledgehammer to crack a walnut."

"So, you're more than willing to kill someone like Luciano, but when it comes to saving a young girl's life, you don't want to get involved. Is that it? What's the matter, not important enough for you, not enough glory for you"

Val was shaking with anger, but he said nothing.

"That's enough," Trena said. "Watching you two is like watching a couple of kids argue over a toy." She turned to Thomes. "I want you to get Benny to set things up, so he'll be ready to trace that call when it comes in. Once we know where they are, Val will go and get the girl. Okay? Right. Get to work," she said as if they had answered her.

They returned to the squad room, neither of them speaking. Once there Thomes briefed the rest of the team with what they knew.

"Benny, I want you to start working on that partial trace. Get Melanie to help you, and I want you to get over to Lever's home and be ready for the next call."

"Yes, sir," Benny said. And he left the squad room.

Thomes turned to Ricardo. "As soon as Benny and Melanie get us something, I want you and Susanne to go check it out okay."

"Yes, boss. No problem."

Benny and Melanie returned to the squad room together.

"We're on our way to Mrs. Lever's house to set up so we can trace the next call when it comes in," Benny said.

"Right," said Thomes. "Get going. As soon as you have anything, call Ricardo or Susanne and give them the details. Okay? And email a recent photo of Sara back here."

"Yes, sir. Will do."

After Benny and Melanie left the office, Thomes turned to Ricardo. "I want you and Susanne to put a team together on standby just in case they get us the address. Be ready to move."

"On it now," Ricardo said.

"So, what do you think?" Ricardo asked Susanne as soon as Thomes left the office.

"What do I think about what?" Susanne replied.

"You know, the little Lever girl. Do you think we have a chance of getting her back alive?"

"I don't see why not. They don't know that Mrs. Lever came to us for help. They won't be expecting us to be involved. We've put a good team together. As soon as we find them, they won't know what hit them."

After a while, Ricardo's phone started ringing. He answered, spoke briefly, and hung up. "That was Benny," Ricardo said to Thomes, who had returned during the short phone call. "He was just checking in. He said they were all set up and ready for when the kidnappers call again."

"Okay," Thomes said. "I'm going back to the director's office. Call me when you hear anything."

Both Ricardo and Susanne were sitting at their desks. The team of agents they had put together was ready to go as soon as Benny and Melanie gave them the location they needed.

Ricardo smiled at her. "You could be right. We should get the girl back safe and sound. Maybe we could go out and celebrate when this is over? If it goes well, that is." He was going to suggest dinner and a movie.

"Yeah, we should speak to Thomes. Try to arrange for us all to go out and celebrate. That's a good idea."

Ricardo looked crestfallen; he had meant that just he and Susanne should go out, not the whole team. He was going to tell her he loved her, and that the way Val treated her wasn't right. He would never treat her that way. But, in the end, he said nothing.

+++

Susanne had a feeling that Ricardo was going to say more—than he was suggesting that just the two of them should go out. She didn't want that, which is why she had suggested they all celebrate together.

Before either of them could say anything else, Ricardo's phone started to ring. *Saved by the bell*, Susanne thought.

Ricardo picked up the phone. "Yes," he said with ill-disguised anger. "Okay. Yes. No, stay where you are. I'll call you back."

"Was that Benny?" Susanne asked.

"Yes. The kidnappers called to give Mrs lever their demands, and Benny and Melanie managed to trace the call. It's a strange address though."

"Strange how?" Susanne asked.

"It's an office block."

"An office block! Are they sure? It seems like a strange place to hold a little girl hostage. Too many people around."

"Yeah, I know. I'm going to call Thomes. See what he thinks."

Ricardo called the director's office and asked to speak to Thomes. He passed on what Benny had told him. "I told both Benny and Melanie to stay where they are for the moment. Susanne and I are taking the van and heading over there now," he said.

+++

"Okay," Thomes said. "Check it out, and we'll join you there." Thomes hung up the phone and turned to the director. "They've found them." He turned to Val. "Come on, Val. We can pick up Benny at the Lever house on the way."

Thomes and Val left the office and picked Benny up on route. "What's happening?" Thomes asked Benny.

"The kidnappers called to say they wanted twenty million dollars. They gave Mrs. Lever the details of where to send the money. They let her speak to Sara—proof of life. They stayed on long enough for us to trace the call. I know it sounds strange, but the trace came back to an office block downtown."

"Okay, thank you," Thomes said. He called Ricardo and asked, "So what have you got?"

"We've had a look around, and if Benny is right, you're not going to like it at all."

"What do you mean, if Benny is right?"

"It's like I said before. An office block to hold a kidnapped child. It just doesn't sound right to me."

"Just stay there and keep your eyes open. We'll be with you in a few minutes," Thomes said.

"So, if this is the right place, then we get to see the great Valentine Frankland in action," Ricardo said to Susanne. They were sitting in an unmarked van outside a large, modern office building. "Then we'll see if he's as good as people keep saying."

"I think you're just jealous," Susanne said. "You saw what happened at the assault course just like the rest of us."

"Yeah, but that was on the assault course. This is real life," Ricardo said.

"Just what have you got against him?" Susanne asked.

Ricardo didn't answer; he just shrugged his shoulders.

When Thomes arrived with Benny and Val, they all got into the back of the van.

"As you can see," Ricardo said. "It's not going to be easy getting in there. If they are in there, they're sure to have someone looking out for trouble, and if they see us, it's game over."

"We're not going in," Thomes said. "Val is going in alone. If the girl is in there, he'll locate and secure her. Once he has her, he'll bring her out. If, however, he runs into any trouble, we'll go in after them. Is that clear?"

"Yes, boss," they all said.

"Right," said Thomes. Meanwhile, Benny had fitted Val with a bullet-proof vest, wired him up with an earwig, and attached a body cam to his vest. "We'll be able to follow everything that happens in there," Thomes said.

"He's all set," Benny said.

"Isn't it a risk sending him without a weapon?" Susanne said. "What happens if they capture him?"

"If he was carrying a weapon, he might well be stopped at the door," Thomes said. "Besides, he doesn't need a weapon—he *is* a weapon."

They all looked at him.

"You've all seen what he can do," Thomes said.

"But what if the kidnappers have guns?" Benny said. "I know he's fast, but he isn't faster than a bullet, and he isn't bulletproof, is he?

"No, he isn't bullet-proof, but he'll be wearing the body armor you fitted him with, won't he?" Thomes said. "So, I'm sure he'll be fine. There is a good chance that they might have guns, but there is also a good chance they won't want to use them. The noise could attract too much attention."

Val exited the van and entered the building, merging with other people who were going in. No one spoke to him or challenged him in any way.

"Okay I'm in," Val said. "I'll start at the bottom and work my way up."

Val made his way down to the basement. As he'd expected, there was nothing there. He then rode the elevator up to the tenth floor. He got out of the elevator and went to the fire door and took the stairs to the next floor. When he got there, he opened the fire door a crack so he could peek through. Seeing nothing, he stepped through into the hallway, his ears straining for any signs of life. He heard the faint sound of someone moving. He peeked around the corner and saw a man dressed in a suit. He was well built, and Val guessed he was about five foot eight. He had a pair of sunglasses perched on his head. Val had to smile as he moved quietly towards the man. Just as Val got close, the man turned towards him. He looked surprised.

+++

As Thomes and the rest of the team listened, they heard a man's voice.

"Here we go," Val said.

"Get ready," Thomes said. "As soon as he gets the girl out, we move in."

"Hey who are you? What are you doing here?" A man's voice was picked up by Val's microphone.

+++

"I'm sorry," Val said to the man standing in the hallway next to a closed door. "I seem to have gone wrong somewhere and got lost. Maybe you can help me."

"What are you looking for?" the man asked.

Val took a piece of paper out his pocket and stepped forward to show the man. As the man looked down at the paper, Val's hand shot out towards the base of the throat. The man was fast. He brought his hands up and blocked Val's blow. They stood for a moment facing each other, and then they circled each other feigning kicks and punches. There was a short tussle, and Val's body-cam was torn off. Val spun around and hit the man in the face with his elbow. The man staggered from the blow. Val struck him firmly behind the ear. The man hit the floor, unconscious. Val opened the door to the room and saw it was empty. He dragged the man inside, secured his limbs with cable ties, and covered his mouth with gaffer tape. He searched the man and found his gun, which he put into his pocket. He saw the man was wearing an earwig. He removed his earwig and replaced it with the one the man had been wearing. He decided to remove his body armor; it was slowing him down. When he saw the camera had been broken, he smiled at himself. Thomes would be pissed. Never mind. He went back to the door. He looked out and saw no one. After a brief look back at the unconscious man, he slipped through the doorway and closed the door behind him. He walked along the hallway listening to chatter through the earwig. It helped to know what the other people were doing. He began checking other rooms along the corridor. In the last room on this floor, he found three more men. Holding them at gunpoint, he made them lie on their bellies. He tied them and gagged them just as he had done to the first man. Once he was sure all the rooms on the floor were clear, he exited through the fire door and went up to the top floor. Even though Val could hear what the other men were saying, he used caution. He thought there were about four more men on the top floor. When he walked through the fire door, he saw a group of three men standing together talking. Val drew his gun and leveled it at them. He walked towards them. "The first one to make a noise dies," Val said.

The men turned to look at Val with identical looks of surprise on their faces.

"Who the fuck are you?" asked the tallest one. "And just what the fuck are you doing here?"

"I'm just passing through," Val said. "But seeing as how I'm here, where's the girl?"

"Fuck you," said the man with the tattoo.

"That's not an option," Val said. "Now I want you all to reach inside your jackets and remove your guns—very slowly—and put them very carefully on the floor. Then I want you all in that room." He pointing to an open door that led into an adjoining room.

The men did as Val told them. Once they were in the room, Val told them all to lie on the floor. "All of you—on the floor on your stomachs!"

"I'm not lying on the floor," the tall man said.

"You either lie down or I'll put you down," Val said.

The men looked at Val, saw the look on his face, and lowered themselves onto the floor. One by one, Val secured them with cable ties as he had done with the others. He put tape over their mouths and left them there. He then continued his search of the other rooms. When he opened the door to the next-to-the-last room on that floor, he saw Sara. She was tied to a chair, and there was tape over her mouth. Her eyes went wide as Val came in and closed the door. Val went to the girl and knelt in front of her. He put his finger to his mouth in a shushing gesture. "Hello there, Sara. My name is Val, and I'm here to take you home to your mommy and daddy. Okay?"

The girl looked terrified, but she nodded.

"Good. Now I'm going to untie you and remove this tape. It might sting a little, but I need you to be brave and not cry out. Okay?"

The girl nodded again. Val pulled the tape off and untied her. She was crying and shaking with fright.

"Right now, I'm going to take you out of here, but I want you to stay close to me—."

Before Val had a chance to say more, the girl screamed. Val turned to see a man standing in the doorway with a gun in his hand. The man fired. Val fell to the floor. Sara continued to scream. Before the man in the doorway could fire again, Val shot him three times in the chest. He fell dead in the doorway. Val turned his attention to Sara. "Hush now, Sara," he said. "It's all right. You're safe now."

"Is he dead?" Sara asked looking at the man lying on the floor.

"Yes, I'm afraid he is. But I had no choice. He would have killed both of us."

"Oh no!" she cried. "You're hurt! Your bleeding!"

"It's nothing serious," he said. "Don't you be worrying about it. We're going to get you home as soon as possible. Your mom is very worried about you."

"They shot my dad," Sara said.

"Yes, I know they did, but he's at the hospital. He's going to be okay."

Sara's face broke into a smile "Really? He's okay? You promise?"

"Yes, I promise," Val said.

Val slid over to the wall near the door and sat there. Sara followed and knelt beside him.

+++

Back in the van, Thomes had been calling Val but getting no response. They had lost video feed after Val's encounter with the first man.

"Is the earwig still working?" Thomes asked Benny.

"Yes. It seems to be working fine," Benny said.

Then they heard gunshots and a girl screaming. The sounds were muffled.

"Shit!" Thomes said. "Benny, get everyone moving. We're going in. Susanne, Ricardo, come on. Let's get in there!" They all went in through the front door, showing their badges to the security guards. When they reached the top floor, they checked each room. They found the three men Val had tied up. They found the dead man who was lying in a doorway. And they found Val sitting against a wall in a pool of blood, the young girl sitting close to him.

"Why the hell didn't you answer me?" Thomes shouted at him.

Val handed him both earwigs. "Sorry. I had to take mine out and use theirs so I could figure out what they were doing."

"Why the hell didn't you let us know?" Thomes snapped at him.

"Because I didn't want to advertise that I was here," Val replied.

"Get an ambulance!" Thomes said. He turned to Susanne. "Get her out of here, will you?" He gestured towards Sara.

"Yes, of course," Susanne said. Then to Sara, she said. "Come on, honey, you come with me."

"But I want to stay here!" Sara said.

"Yes, I know you do, but we have to let the paramedics fix Val up. We'll wait downstairs for him, okay?"

"Sara nodded and left the room with Susanne.

"You guys missed a great party," Val said. "But I saved you some turkeys. You'll find three of them in one of the rooms further down, plus there are some on the floor below trussed and ready for roasting."

Thomes sent Ricardo to check. He came back and told Thomes what he had found.

"Only one dead?" Thomes said. "You must be slipping. Or maybe just getting soft in your old age. You left most of them alive. That's not like you."

"Yeah, I know. I must be slipping. Or maybe you've had a bad influence on me."

The paramedics arrived. They put Val on a gurney, took him down in the elevator, and wheeled him out towards the ambulance. Sara and Susanne were waiting in the lobby for him.

"Hey, Sara," said Val, "I thought you'd be eager to be on your way home."

"I wanted to wait and see you and to say thank you. My mom is coming here to pick me up. Are you going to be all right?"

"Yes, I'm going to be fine. It's just a flesh wound. Really. Nothing for you to worry about."

The paramedics loaded Val into the back of the ambulance. "Is anyone going with him?" They asked.

Susanne wanted to go, but only she and Sara had come down. Everyone else was still on the top floor. She knew she couldn't leave Sara alone until her mom arrived or someone else came down. So she told them they would follow later.

"Okay," said the one who seemed to be in charge. And they drove away.

+++

When they arrived at the hospital, Val was taken for X-rays, and then he was sent to a cubical to wait for a doctor to give him the results.

"You are a very lucky man, Mr. Frankland," reported the doctor when he finally arrived. "The bullet passed straight through the fleshy part of your arm without hitting the bone. Now, you'll have some pain, but we'll give you something for that. The nurse will be in soon, and we'll clean, stitch, and dress the wound. You'll have to keep your arm in a sling for a few days. Rest the arm and try not to move it more than you have to, or you might start it bleeding again."

"Thank you, doctor," Val said.

After the doctor left, Thomes and the rest of the team came in.

"I'll be fine," Val told them. "It's nothing serious."

"The next time you disobey a direct order, I will shoot you myself," said Thomes. "Do you understand me?"

"Yes, sir," Val said.

"Now you can explain to me what happened to your camera," ordered Thomes. "And why you removed your body armor. Also, you can explain why you removed that earpiece."

"I've already told you," Val said. "I removed my earwig so I could use the one I took from the first man. I needed to hear what the rest of the men on the top floor were doing. That vest was slowing me down, so I took it off."

"You should have told me what you were doing, but no—you had to play the hero again, didn't you?" Thomes said. "Now it seems that you made quite an impression on young Sara. So much so that she had her mom bring her here to make sure you're all right. If you don't mind, they would like to come in and see you."

"Okay. Let them come in," Val said.

Sara ran straight to Val and hugged him. "Are you all right?" she asked.

"Yes, I'm fine. The nurse is going to bandage me up, and then I'll be as good as new." Val looked at the tall, elegant blond woman standing in the doorway. The resemblance between this woman and young Sara was unmistakable. "Is this your mom?"

"Yes," Sara said.

The woman stepped forward. "I want to thank you for saving my daughter's life," she said.

"It was my pleasure," Val said. "As long as Sara is okay, that's all that matters."

"What about you, Mr. Frankland? How badly are you hurt?"

"It's not as bad as it looks. It's just a flesh wound. Nothing to worry about."

"Well, I would like to thank you once again on behalf of me and my husband. We will both be forever in your debt." She had tears in her eyes. "If there is ever anything we can do to repay you, just say the word."

"Thank you. But seeing Sara safe is payment enough."

"Well, goodbye, Mr. Frankland. And once again, thank you. Come on, Sara, let's go home." Sara took her mother's hand, and they left.

"Well that worked out well," Val said.

"Worked out well!" spat Thomes. "Just what the hell did you think you were doing in there?"

"What do you mean, what was I doing? I was doing my job."

"No! Your job was to find the girl and get her out. If you ran into problems, you were supposed to wait for backup! But, no! You had to do it your way, didn't you? Ignoring orders and playing the hero again. I should have known."

"Look," Val said. "I assessed the situation, and in my opinion, sitting and waiting for you was putting Sara in danger, so I decided to get her out."

"A decision that could have gotten both of you killed."

"But it didn't, did it?"

"No, not this time. But it did get you a bullet through your arm. Just who you think you are—fucking Roger Ramjet or something? It could just as easily have been the girl who got shot. You are reckless. You are careless. And you are dangerous. Just as soon as I get back to the office, I am officially requesting that you be removed from this assignment and replaced with someone who can at least follow orders!" With that, Thomes turned and left the room.

CHAPTER 6

Val's Goodbye

Val was struggling to get dressed. He had managed to get his shirt on and fastened before the nurse put his arm in a sling. When Susanne came in, he was trying to put his jacket on. She stood watching him for a few minutes then she started laughing. "Do you need any help with that?" she asked.

"Help would be nice," he said. "But just what is so funny?"

"Just watching you," she said. "It looks like you're rehearsing some new kind of breakdance routine."

Val smiled. "Maybe I am. Now are you going to help me or are you just going to stand there laughing?"

Susanne looked up into his face. "I guess I have you at my mercy while you're like this."

"Yeah, it sure looks that way, doesn't it? So, the question is, what are you going to do about it?" She put her arms around his neck and kissed him. "Thank you. But what was that for?"

"That is part of my new interrogation technique," she said.

"Hmm … I don't think I've come across this method before. Is this a common form of interrogation?"

"No," she said. "It's only used in special cases, but when I heard that you would be a tough nut to crack, I thought I had better think of something different. I knew I might need a new interrogation technique if I'm ever to crack you."

"You know, I'm not sure it's working. I think I might need some more interrogation."

"Come on, fool," she said as she helped him with his jacket.

"So, is that it? Is that interrogation over?" he asked.

"For now," she said. "We'll have to wait to see how you behave. If you're good, I might have to continue with the interrogation later, but for now, we will just have to wait and see."

"Yeah, I suppose we will," he said.

"So, I guess this means our date tonight is off," she said.

He looked at her. "Are you canceling on me?"

"No, not at all. I just thought that you might not want to go out with your arm in a sling that's all."

"This is nothing serious. It's just a flesh wound. And I've been looking forward to going out with you again. Just think of all the sympathy I can get."

"You fool," she said. "Come on. I'll take you back to the office. Do you think Thomes meant what he said about getting you taken off this assignment?"

"I think he'll try."

"Why does he hate you so much?"

"Oh, I think hate is a bit strong. He loves me."

"He sure has a strange way of showing it."

"I know it seems like that, but you just don't know him the way I do."

"No, I don't suppose I do."

When they got back to the office, Melanie and Doc were waiting for them. Melanie went straight to Val. "Oh, my God, I thought Ricardo was messing with us when he said you'd been shot."

"It's nothing to worry about. Just a flesh wound."

"What the hell happened?" Doc asked. "Thomes came back like a bear with a sore head. He went straight up to the director's office. As far as I know, he's still there."

"Yeah, that figures," Val said. "He's pissed at me because I didn't follow his plan. I was the one there. I had to make the call to change his precious plan to get the girl out safe."

"So, what do you think will happen now?" Melanie asked.

"I don't know," Val said. "I suppose we will have to see what Trena says."

The phone rang, and everyone turned to look at it. It was Ricardo who answered it. "Yes, he's just arrived with Susanne. Okay, I will." He hung up and turned to the others. "That was the director. She wants Val to go to her office now."

"Okay. Here we go. I'll see you later."

"If we're spared," Melanie finished for him.

Val smiled and left the squad room.

+++

Val made his way to the director's office and went in after a quick knock on the door. "You wanted to see me?" he asked.

"Yes, I did," Trena said. "I want you to tell me just what the hell happened out there today."

"Sure," he said. "No problem. What happened was that we got a little girl safely back to her mom. And once her dad has fully recovered, they will be a happy family again. Plus, just as a bonus, we got some bad guys locked up. That is what happened."

"So, I suppose that, in your mind, you think that the outcome gives you some sort of special privilege and the right to just ignore orders. Agent Thomes gave you specific orders, and you just totally ignored them."

Val looked at Trena. "Yes, I did, but it was your idea to send me in there in the first place to get that girl, and I was the one on the ground. In my opinion—not that it seems to be worth much around here— waiting around for Thomes and his merry band to come blundering in would have put both the girl and me in more danger, so I made the decision to get her out of there myself."

"And in the process, you got shot," Trena said.

"Yes, I did. But if you were listening to what I said, you'd know that, if I had waited for Thomes and his band of gung-ho heroes, both of us could have been killed. So, in my humble opinion, it was worth it."

"But what would have happened if that bullet had been a few inches to the right? The bullet could just have easily hit you in the chest instead of your arm. Then both of you could have been dead."

Val smiled. "But it wasn't, and we aren't. She is alive and well."

"Yes, she is, but I'm still supporting Agent Thomes's request to have you replaced. He is right. You are reckless, and you are dangerous. You can go commit suicide somewhere else."

"And just what the hell is that supposed to mean?"

"You know full well what it means," Trena said.

"I don't have a clue. But there is one thing I suspected, and now it has become quite clear to me: you didn't want me here to start with! But seeing as how it was you and Thomes who sent for me, you had to put up with me, so you sent me on a job that even Thomes's monkeys could have done. Now, because I did it in a way you didn't like, and because I didn't get myself and Sara killed, you're trying to hang this around my neck as a failure and use it to get rid of me. Well, fuck you—all of you! And I wish you the best of luck getting me replaced. Now, if you've quite finished, I am going back to my hotel to get some rest, just like the doctor ordered. But you be sure to let me know how this turns out, won't you? You know where I am if you need me." Val turned on his heel and walked out of the office, leaving Thomes and Trena looking after him.

+++

Thomes went back down to the squad room and looked around. "Doesn't anyone have any work to do?" he snapped at them.

"Where's Val?" Melanie asked.

"He's not here," Thomes.

"Yeah, I can see that. But where is he?"

"Look," Thomes said. "He's not here, and that is that. Now get back to work unless you want to join him at the unemployment office."

They all looked at Thomes, but no one spoke. *Oh, yes,* thought Ricardo, *there is a god. What a good day.* All he'd had to do was wait until Val fucked up, and it looked as if he had done so—royally. Ricardo felt like dancing a jig. He was so happy he thought he might even kiss Thomes.

+++

Melanie and Susanne were in the ladies' room.

"So where are you going tonight?" Melanie asked.

"I don't know yet, but I think it might just be dinner and a few drinks. I don't think he'll want to go dancing, do you?"

"Oh, I don't know. You can never tell with him. You seem a bit down, a bit sad. I thought you would be happy."

"I am happy. It's just that Thomes seems to have made good on his threat to get rid of Val. And even if he hasn't, once Val does whatever was he was brought here to do, he'll leave. Either way, the result will be the same. So, what do I do? I like him, but would I be just another notch on his bedpost? If you know what I mean?"

"Yes, I know just what you mean," Melanie said. "Have you told him how you feel?"

"God no. I thought if I started saying things like 'I think I love you' on the first date, there might not be a second one. But whether we were dancing or just sat talking, I looked around and saw the look of envy, and I knew it was because I was with Val. Do you know what I mean?"

"Yes," Melanie said, "I know exactly what you mean. He's always been like a big brother to me, but I still know just what you mean."

"How come the two of you never got together?" Susanne asked.

Melanie smiled. "As I told you, he's always been like a big brother to me. He saved me from that nasty fate I told you about—when I was young—and he's been there for me ever since. If I ever need him, all I have to do is call him. He used to tell the local boys, 'Touch my sister, and I will kick your ass.' It was difficult for me to get dates! The boys used to go to Val to get his permission to ask me out."

Susanne smiled. "I bet that was fun."

"It was. But I never had to worry about boys pushing their luck with me, if you know what I mean."

Susanne laughed at the thought of the local boys going to Val to ask his permission to ask Melanie out. "I think I do. I was thinking about something that Ricardo said earlier."

"And what did Ricardo have to say?"

"He said that guys like Val arrive on the scene and then disappear just as quickly, leaving broken hearts behind them so someone else has to pick up the pieces."

"I think Ricardo is full of shit. He's just jealous because he fancies you, and you like Val."

Susanne looked surprised. "Really?"

"Yes. You like Val a lot, I know that, so make the most of your time with him. Think about what I said—tell him how you feel. You might be surprised at the result."

"Okay, I will," she said.

Susanne thought about her upcoming date with Val. Maybe she should just tell him it was off and try to forget him, but she knew she couldn't do that. She would keep her date. She would try to tell him how she felt and see what happened. If he wasn't interested in a long-term relationship, at least she would know.

+++

Trena Kennedy was at home preparing dinner. She was thinking about what had happened earlier with Val. It shouldn't have surprised her; she knew as well as Thomes did what he was like. She was just sitting down to eat when her doorbell rang. She opened her door to find Val standing there. "Val? What are you doing here?"

"I was just passing, and I thought I would call and see if you've submitted the request to have me replaced yet."

She laughed. "Why is that? Have you come to say sorry and ask me not to?"

"You should know me better than that," he said. "No, I brought you this to save you the trouble." He handed her an envelope.

She took it and looked at him her eyebrows arched. "What's this?"

"Can't you guess?"

Trena looked at him. For a moment she said nothing. "You're joking, right?"

"No, it's no joke. It's my resignation. I've already sent a copy to headquarters. I was going to give it to you this morning, but things happened, and we got a bit sidetracked, didn't we?"

Trena looked from the envelope in her hand to Val. "Why? I've never known you quit anything before. So tell me why?"

Val shrugged. "I suppose there's a first time for everything. Besides, I thought you would just be happy to see me gone. At least this way you don't have to try to explain why you want me out. There'll be no arguing about it with the boys upstairs who wanted me here in the first place. Just bye-bye annoying problem. Anyway, I'm sorry for disturbing you. I'll go and leave you in peace." He pointed to the envelope in her hand. "Maybe I've made your evening, maybe not; either way it doesn't matter. We might see each other again; we might not. I think the latter will make you and Agent Thomes very happy."

"You have it all wrong," she said. "You know it's never been like that, not really."

"Yeah, I guess maybe I do." He turned to walk away.

"Have you told Susanne you've resigned?" she called after him.

Val turned back to her. "Is there anyone left who doesn't know about Susanne and me? And no, I haven't told her yet. I was planning on telling her tonight over dinner. Why?"

"I think Thomes might not know. She does look a lot like Juliet, doesn't she? Where are you taking her tonight?"

"I've made reservations at Cityzen I know she likes it there. I thought I would tell her over dinner. And, yes, she is a lot like Juliet, and not just in looks. There are a thousand other little things as well."

"Yes, I know. You look after her. She's in love with you, did you know that?"

It was Val's turn to look surprised. "No, I didn't. But how do you know?"

"A woman knows these things."

"Okay. And you don't have to worry. I'll take very good care of her. I think the chances of you and me meeting again are slim, but you never know, do you?"

Trena stood there for a moment longer watching as he walked away. She was shocked; this was something she had not expected. She, like Thomes, had known Val for many years. She had expected him to fight her over her decision to have him removed. But wasn't there something different about him? Something had changed, and she thought she knew what had caused that change. She had told Val that Susanne was in love with him. But she had not said that she thought he was in love with her. She would talk to Thomes about this and ask if he thought the same. She watched until Val was out of sight. Then she went back inside smiling.

CHAPTER 7

Time for Change

When Val arrived at Susanne's apartment to pick her up, she invited him in to wait while she finished getting ready. Val looked around. It was a good-sized apartment. The floor was covered in deep plush carpet, and the living room was furnished with an expensive-looking leather recliner and a sofa. One wall was filled with books. They were not the sort of books Val liked; he saw a lot of romance novels there. On the coffee table, there was a vase with fresh flowers. The kitchen was spotless—a place for everything and everything in its place. Susanne came out of the bedroom, and Val looked at her. "You have a beautiful home," he said.

"Thank you. I'm glad you like it. While I was starting to get ready I wondered whether or not you would turn up."

"And why would you wonder that?"

"Well with all that happened today … and then Thomes said you were at the unemployment office." Val surprised her by laughing. "And just what is so funny?"

"Sorry, but the look on your face. I'm willing to bet that, as Thomes was saying all this, he was storming around and telling everyone to get back to work—even if you were all working—or you would be joining me at this office, right?"

"Yes, that was just what he was like. But how did you know that?"

"Because I know Thomes, and I know what he's like."

"So, you're not fired then?"

"Enough about work," he said. "Are you ready for some dinner?"

"Of course, but I still don't understand."

"Don't understand what?" Val grinned.

"Arghhh! I give up!"

"That's good because I'm hungry. Come on, let's go."

She flapped her hands at him. "Okay, let's go get you some food. So where are we going?"

Val took her hand raised to his lips and kissed it. "I thought that since you enjoyed last night we would go back to Cityzen."

"Are you sure? It's very expensive."

"Yes, I'm sure. And you are worth it. I managed to get a table."

"You're full of surprises!"

They went to the restaurant where a very attentive maître d' guided them to their table. They ordered their meals, and when the food arrived, Susanne just sat looking at Val.

"What?" he asked. "Is there something hanging from my nose?"

"No, nothing like that. I was just wondering how your arm is."

"It's fine," he said. "Why?"

"Oh, I was just wondering if you need help cutting up your food. Do you want me to feed you?"

He smiled at her. "You must be reading my mind. But I thought you might not want to get into that in public."

She flushed. "Maybe next time," she said.

"I'll look forward to that."

Once the meal was over, they left the restaurant and went to a café bar where Val spoke to a waiter. She saw a note change hands, and they were guided to a table. They ordered drinks and were talking about things in general. Val was going to tell her that he had resigned so that he could be with her. He would ask her if she wanted to be with him. He would tell her he liked her a lot. No, he not only like her, no he would tell her the truth, tell her that he was in love with her, and if she said she felt the same, and that she would like to be with him, he would tell her everything. If she didn't, then he would …. He would what? That was a good question. What exactly would he do? He would cross that bridge when he got to it. He had just started to speak when Melanie, Benny, and Ricardo came in.

+++

"Hi there," Melanie said. "We were just out for a few drinks and we saw you. We thought we'd stop and say hello. You don't mind, do you?"

"Not at all," Susanne said. "It's good to see you."

"Yeah, drag up a stool and sit," Val said.

So, they sat down with Val and Susanne for a while. They drank with them and talked about things in general. Ricardo kept trying to get Susanne to dance with him, but she said she was too tired, and she stayed seated. Melanie said that the three of them were going to a night club and asked if Val and Susanne wanted to join them. They both said thanks but no thanks. The three of them finally left, leaving Val and Susanne alone again. When the evening was over, Val took Susanne home.

"Would you like to come in for a coffee?" Susanne asked.

"Thank you. Yes, that would be nice."

Val took a seat in Susanne's living room while she went into the kitchen. She came back into the room and said. "Sorry, I don't seem to have any coffee."

"That's okay. I don't drink it."

She just looked at him, and then they both started laughing. Val stood and opened his arms.

"How's your arm?" she asked.

"Why don't you come over here and find out?"

She stepped forward into the circle of his arms, and they closed around her. She tilted her face up to him. His lips found hers, and nothing else mattered. She took his hand and led him into the bedroom. They made love and then lay snuggled up together.

"Can I ask you something?" Susanne whispered.

"Sure. Anything."

"What is Ralph?"

He propped himself up on his good arm, looked at her, and started laughing.

"And just what is so funny?" she asked sounding hurt.

He kissed her. "You," he said. "You looked so serious."

"No one will tell me anything, and it's so frustrating."

"Well, it comes from a story I read as a kid. I don't remember where I read it. I think it was in one of those boy's magazines, but I loved the story. It was about a family who moved from one side of the country to the other, but somehow their dog got left behind. Then, after about a year, the dog showed up at their new home. It had crossed the country all alone to find its master. I just loved that story. It just sort of called to me. You know what I mean?"

"Yes, I know what you mean."

"The dog, as you might have guessed, was called Ralph. So, after that, when something amazing or unbelievable happened, we would say it's 'Ralph'."

"So, earlier today, when you said it was Ralph, what did you mean?"

"I meant that something amazing or unbelievable had happened."

"You're doing it again."

"Doing what?"

"Talking in riddles, and I don't know what you mean. Why won't you just give me a straight answer?"

"You asked about Ralph, and I told you."

"So, does that mean you'll be leaving again soon?"

"What? Leaving? Don't tell me *you* want to get rid of me as well."

"You know you can be such an ass," she said.

"Yeah, I know. I've been told that many times."

"Well, why don't you go be an ass somewhere else?" she flung at him.

"All right," he said. "If that's the way you want it, I will."

He got out of bed and got dressed. He went out of the bedroom and picked up his coat. He looked back at the bedroom door opened his mouth to speak then closed it again. What would be the point? This was probably the best. He stepped outside and closed the door behind him.

After a few minutes, Susanne got off the bed and went to the door. She meant to call him back to say sorry, even if it wasn't her fault. She had meant to tell him that she loved him. But it was too late; he was gone. She went back into the bedroom and threw herself onto the bed. Why had she told him to go? She didn't know. It wasn't supposed to be like this. She was going to tell him how she felt—that she was in love with him—but then everything had gone wrong, and now he was gone. She picked up the phone, and before she could stop herself, she had dialed Melanie's number. Melanie answered almost immediately.

"I'm sorry about this," Susanne said through her tears. "I didn't mean to wake you."

"You didn't wake me. I've just got in. What's wrong?"

Susanne told her everything. She had to repeat a few things because she was crying so much. "I just had to talk to someone. Do you have any idea where he might go?"

"He could have gone anywhere, but if he turns up here, I'll call you, okay?"

"Thank you so much," Susanne said. "I'm sorry to trouble you with this."

"It's no trouble at all. That's what friends are for. Have you tried Thomes?"

"God, no. I thought they hated each other."

"No, they don't hate each other. I know it might seem like it, but when they were younger, they were very close. Val might have gone back to his hotel. If he didn't, he might have gone to Doc's I suppose."

"Do you think so?"

"I'll try both. Doc's been like a father to him. I'll check both of them out if you like."

"Would you please? I feel so stupid." Susanne was still crying, but her sobs had tapered off. "It was all my fault."

"Stop that right now," Melanie said sharply. "You forget that I know Val a lot better than you do, and I am willing to bet that he was as much to blame as you, if not more. Now you try to get some sleep while I try to find him. If I do find him, I'll call you, okay? By the way, have you tried his cell phone?"

"No point. He left it behind."

"Okay. You try to get some sleep, and I'll get back to you."

"Thank you so much," Susanne said. "I'll try to sleep, but I have never felt less like sleeping in my life."

"I know. But at least try to rest, and I'll be in touch as soon as I find anything out."

They said goodbye. Susanne disconnected the call and lay on her bed crying. She felt as if her heart would break.

+++

Thomes had gone back to the office. He walked into the squad room and saw Val sitting at his desk. "What are you doing here? I thought you were out with Susanne?"

"How do you know about that? It was supposed to be a secret."

"You, of all people, should know there are no secrets—not around here."

"Yeah, I suppose your right. Well, I was out with Susanne, and now I'm here. I thought I would catch up with my paperwork and make sure everything was in order before I leave. Have you spoken to Trena?"

"Yes, I have. She told me that you handed in your resignation. Now you tell me why. In all the years I've known you, I have never known you to back away from anything, and now you're quitting. So why? Is it because I was asking to have you replaced? Or was it because of the incident at the assault course?"

Val laughed. "No, it has nothing to do with either of those things, and you of all people should know better than to suggest that. The thing with the assault course was nothing—probably just a glitch. And besides, I've gotten used to people trying to kill me over the years. And as for you and Trena trying to get rid of me, I've sort of got used to that as well."

"So, tell me why."

"Okay. Susanne is why. She has made me see what I want—that she is what I want—and I can't keep doing this if I want to be with her. Even the great Roger Ramjet gets tired sometimes. Plus, you can't get me fired if I don't work here, can you?"

"You just don't give up, do you?"

"Why change now and break the habit of a lifetime?"

"So, are you going to stick around? Or are you going to run again?"

"I would have thought you would just be happy to get rid of me. So why the sudden interest in where I'm going and what I'm going to do?"

"I have my reasons. Now tell me, why are you quitting?"

"You want to know?"

Thomes nodded. "I wouldn't have asked if I didn't."

"Okay," Val said. "I've had enough, and I'm tired. When I close my eyes to try to sleep, I can see all the faces of all the people I've killed. It's taken me a long time, but I've finally figured out that I've become a version of the men I've been hunting all these years, and I just can't do it anymore. I suppose I just needed someone to make me see it."

"You mean Susanne?"

Val shrugged. "As the old song says, it doesn't matter anymore, does it, my old friend?"

"So tell me what's happening with you two?"

"Nothing is happening with us two."

"What happened?"

Val sighed. "It's me. I suppose I'm what happened. She told me I was an ass, and I said I had been told that before. So she told me to go and be an ass somewhere else. And here I am being an ass."

"So, what are you going to do?"

"I'll finish up here, submit all my reports, make sure everything is in order, and then I will make everybody happy and take my act and put it on the road. You know—put an egg in my shoe and beat it. Pick your metaphor."

"Thanks for that," Thomes said. "But I don't think it's going to make Susanne very happy."

"Yeah, well, I wouldn't be too sure about that."

"So, do have any idea of where you'll go or what you're going to do?"

"I don't know yet. I haven't thought that far ahead. Do you think I'm too old to run away and join the circus?" Val laughed.

"Still a smart arse," Thomes said.

"Yeah, well, I'm too old to change now."

"I think you would fit right in," Thomes said. "The circus is always looking for clowns."

"Yeah, that's what I hear."

Thomes nodded. "Right. Come on."

"Come on where?"

"You need a drink," Thomes said. "And since drinking alone is never a good idea, I suggest you get your coat, and we'll go for a couple of beers."

"Are you still working on that old motorbike of yours?"

"No, I sold that years ago. Now I have a new old motorbike."

"Okay," Val said. "I'll just get my Susanne." There was a look of surprise on Val's face. "Sorry. I meant I'll get my coat."

"I see," Thomes said.

"And what is that supposed to mean?"

"Oh, I think you know exactly what I mean. Did you think I hadn't noticed how much she looks like Juliet? You can tell yourself it's for the best, but you can only fool yourself for so long, my friend. Does she know that you've handed in your resignation?"

"No, I don't think so. I haven't told her."

"Maybe you should."

"What would be the point? It's too late now. Anyway, I thought you wanted to get rid of me."

"Yeah, I did, but you know how it is."

"Don't you go getting all mushy on me," Val said.

"You don't have to worry about that. But, despite what people think, I never hated you. I was angry at you for leaving us. You were the best damn investigator I've ever known. You should have stayed here with us."

"I know you think I made a mistake moving to the other side, but I just got so frustrated bringing the bad guys in only to see those incompetent fools in the courts to let them go again."

"Come on, let's go get that drink."

"Yeah, good idea," Val said. "Things might look better after a couple of drinks. So, come on, Dex, tell me what you're really up to."

"I'm not up to anything, and I've told you not to call me Dex."

Val thought back to when they were young. It had been Val and Dex, the young heart breakers. Then Thomes was shaking him.

"You're doing it again," Thomes said.

"Doing what?"

"Zoning out on me. Going into your little world."

"Yeah, I know, but it's okay. They know me there."

"What the hell are you talking about?"

"Don't ask me. I'm fucked if I know." Val began to laugh.

"I'm getting worried about you."

"Yeah, well, that makes two of us," Val said. "Now if we're going to get those drinks, then let's go get those drinks."

As they made their way out of the building, Thomes thought about how mad he had been when Val had shown up and how much he had wanted to get rid of him again. Now he had to try to find a way to make him stay. Susanne wanted Val; that was obvious. He supposed she was in love with him, or at least she thought she was. Thomes was very fond of Miss Susanne Wilder. Like Val, he had done a double-take when he saw her the first time. The resemblance to his late sister was uncanny.

"Is that a phone ringing?" Val asked.

"Let it ring," Thomes answered.

+++

The phone that had been ringing had indeed been Thomes's, but his calls had been diverted to Ricardo. Melanie was looking for Val. She asked Ricardo if he'd seen Val, and she asked where Tomes was. Ricardo said he would try to find Val as well, but he had no idea where Thomes was.

Melanie tried Thomes's cell phone, but that was off, so she called Trena to ask if she had seen or heard from either of them. Melanie told her about what had happened and how she had been trying to find Val without success. "I've tried his hotel, but he's not there. I've even called Doc to ask if Val went there, but he hasn't seen him or Thomes."

"Are you sure they're together?" Trena asked.

"No, I just thought there was a chance they might be."

"Leave it with me," Trena said. "I think I might be able to find at least one of them. And if they are together, I will let you know, okay?"

"Thanks," Melanie said, and she hung up.

Trena was right in thinking they would go to a bar if they were together. Then they would go back to Thomes's house for a few more drinks. If they were together, Thomes would probably talk Val's ears off about that old motorbike he was rebuilding. She smiled at the thought of how many times she and Thomes had done just that. She would get so drunk she'd fall asleep on a futon Thomes kept in the corner. She got in her car and drove to the bar she thought most likely. They weren't there, but she asked the bartender if he had seen them. He said that Thomes had been in earlier with a friend. They'd had a few drinks and then left. She thanked him and set off for Thomes's house. *Well, at least they're together*, she thought, and it didn't sound as if they were trying to kill each other. When she arrived at Thomes's house, all the lights were on, and there was loud music playing. She went through the unlocked front door and walked into the living room. She turned the music off. She found Thomes asleep on the futon, just as she thought she might, but there was no sign of Val. She looked around the rest of the house, but there was no sign of Val. She went back to where Thomes was still sleeping and started shaking him. "Wake up!" she shouted.

Thomes woke, but slowly. "Stop shaking me," he said. "What do you want?"

"Where's Val?"

"He probably went to bed. He was shitfaced."

"No, he didn't. He's not in the house at all. I looked."

Thomes was mostly awake now. "He said he was leaving this morning, so maybe he got an early start."

"Not if he was as bad off as you say he was."

Thomes thought for a moment. "He said something about the sunrise. We should check if his gear is in his car."

"Where is his car?" Trena asked.

"It's in the drive. You must have walked past it."

"No, it's not there. My car's the only one in the drive."

Thomes went upstairs and found Val's stuff still there. "God damn it," he said. "He must have gone off somewhere."

"But if he was as bad as you say he was, then he can't have gone far."

"If the local police saw him, they would have stopped him for sure. I'll give them a ring to see if they have him."

Thomes made the call and spoke to the local police chief, who told him it had been a very quiet night and they hadn't picked up anyone at all. He took the details describing Val's car and said he would tell his officers to keep an eye out for him. Thomes thanked him and hung up. "No joy there. I can't think of where he could have gone."

"You don't think he could have had an accident, do you?"

"No," he said. "If he'd been in an accident, the police would probably have been informed. I can call the local police back and ask if they've heard anything. We can call the hospital as well if you like." Thomes called the local hospital with no luck.

"So, where the hell can he have taken himself off to?" Trena asked

"I'm not sure," Thomes said. "But he can't be that far away."

CHAPTER 8

Graveyard Shift

"Let's get back to the office," Thomes said. "We can try to find him from there. But you know what he's like—if he doesn't want to be found ..."

"Yes, I know. But why would he be hiding? And why did he go off the way he did? But, considering the state he's in, he should be easy to find."

When they got to the squad room they found the rest of the team already there. "What are you guys doing here at this time?" Thomes asked.

"When Melanie called us looking for Val, we thought you might need a little help," Benny said.

"Have you found him?" Susanne asked.

"No, not yet," Thomes said. "But that doesn't mean much. Like I said to the director if he doesn't want to be found he, he won't be found. Susanne, can I talk to you in my office for a moment."

Susanne followed Thomes into his office and closed the door behind them. "What's this about?" she asked.

"I need to ask you what happened last night."

"What do you mean what happened last night?"

"Look, I know you were out with Val last night. Something happened, and he left you and came here. This is where I found him. He seems to think that you don't want anything more to do with him."

"I didn't say I didn't want anything to do with him. I just told him if he was going to be an ass, he should go be an ass somewhere else. Do you have any idea where he might be?"

"No, not yet. But I will find him. You can be sure of that."

"I thought you said he couldn't be found if he didn't want to be."

Thomes smiled. "Yes, I did. But I know Val very well, and I don't think he will be hiding from us. I do think, however, that he is hurting. Not that he would ever admit it. He's probably gone off to clear his head and think things through. So, tell me what happened."

"I'm not sure," she said. "We went out for dinner and then we went on to a café bar. We were just talking when Melanie, Benny, and Ricardo came in and joined us for a while. Then we went back to my place." Her face reddened as she said this. "I asked him about Ralph, and he told me the story."

"Did he tell you what he meant the other day when he said 'it's Ralph'?"

"No, he didn't. And when I tried to ask him about it, he started avoiding the question. I guess I got angry with him and told him to go be an ass somewhere else. And that's it."

Thomes smiled again. "I know Val very well, and I can tell you that, when he said it's Ralph, he was referring to meeting you."

Susanne looked at him with her mouth open. She shook herself. "Why didn't he just say so instead of all this messing about?"

"Because, my dear, he usually keeps people at arm's length. You are the only person who has got close to him in a long time, and suddenly he is unsure of himself and maybe a little scared. So, he tried to make you push him away—to tell him to go be an ass somewhere else. And it seems he was successful."

Susanne opened her mouth to speak but was cut off by the phone ringing. It was one of the police officers on patrol who had been keeping his eyes open for Val. "We found your man's car," he said.

"Is he with it?" Thomes asked.

"No, he's nowhere to be seen, but there is a lot of blood in and around the car. If it all belongs to your man, he's either in a lot of trouble or he's dead."

"Okay. Thank you. We would like to take the lead on this if you don't mind."

"I don't mind at all. I kind of figured you might want to."

"Please keep on searching. We're on our way."

"We'll keep looking," the police officer continued. "I've asked for the dogs to be brought in, so if you've got something you know for sure is his, that will help."

"No problem," Thomes said. "We'll be there as quickly as we can." He hung up and turned to Susanne. "Come on." They went back into the squad room where Thomes spoke to the whole team. "Right. As you all know, Val disappeared, and we don't know where he went. The police have just called to say they found his car."

"Is he with it?" Melanie asked hopefully.

"No," Thomes said. "They don't know where he is, but they found a lot of blood in and around his car. Now I don't want anyone jumping to any conclusions. We don't know anything yet." He turned to Melanie. "We'll get a sample to you as soon as we can."

"I'm coming with you," she said.

"What good will that do?" Thomes asked her. "We need you here to type the blood as quickly as possible, and you can't do that if you're out there with us."

"It can't be his blood," Melanie said.

"Why not?" Ricardo asked.

"Because it just can't be. God wouldn't allow it, that's all."

"Right, people. Let's move out," Thomes said.

"You will find him? Won't you?" Melanie asked.

"You can count on it," Thomes said.

Melanie hugged Susanne. "Don't you worry. Thomes will find him, and everything will be all right. You'll see."

Susanne hugged her back. "Thank you. I hope so."

+++

Ricardo could not believe all this bullshit. He had worked very hard to find a way to get rid of that arrogant shithead, Val. Just when he thought he had succeeded here they all were running around trying to find him again. He couldn't believe that Thomes and the director wanted to find him; he thought they wanted him gone just as much as he did. But with all the blood the police said they found, he must surely be dead. With a bit of luck, things could then go back to the way they were before Val showed up, and Susanne would be his at last.

+++

Val heard Thomes talking, but it sounded more like gibberish than actual words. When he realized that Thomes was talking in his sleep, he decided he would go out for a walk. He managed to get himself out of the house, but he seemed to be having trouble making his legs do what he wanted, so, in his drunken state, he thought it made sense to drive. He got into his car, but he didn't have a lot of luck with that either. He was driving very slowly and erratically towards the cemetery. His idea had been to visit Juliet's grave. He would sit and watch the sunrise, and he would talk to her for a while. It had been a long time since he'd done that. He would try to explain to her why he had become what he had become and why he had done all the things that he had done. He would tell her he was sorry, and he would tell her how much he missed her. He would tell her he had quit. He would tell her about Susanne and try to explain to her how he felt. He would ask her what he should do. He thought maybe Juliet would understand and maybe even approve of Susanne. Susanne had taken over his thoughts and turned his life upside down, and all it had taken was a smile. When he was quite near the gates of the cemetery, he came back from his memories, and when he looked up, he saw two men standing in front of his car. He slammed on the breaks and came to a screeching halt. "Hey, you bloody idiots! Are you trying to get yourselves killed?"

One of the men approached him. Val rolled down the window and looked up at him. "Hey, man, what are you doing?" Val was about to tell the men to shift out of the way when the man lunged forward through the car window and hit him twice in the stomach. Then both men ran away. At first, Val thought he just been punched in the gut, but then he realized he was bleeding. *You must be getting slow, old buddy,* he said to himself.

He opened the car door and fell out. The pain was massive. *Doesn't look like I'm going to get a chance to say sorry to Susanne,* he thought, and then for no reason, he began to laugh. "You have lost it," he said aloud. Even though the laughter was causing him a lot of pain, he couldn't stop. The more he laughed, the faster the blood pumped out of him. Eventually, he got a measure of control of himself. He had to get to the cemetery. He had to try to get to Juliet. *Concentrate*, he told himself. *God damn it, concentrate! Get a grip!* He closed his eyes and forced himself to focus, but it was so hard. He made himself get moving. At last, he made it to Juliet's grave. "Hello, my love. I made it," he said as he lay down. He felt tired. He would rest for a moment, and then he would see how badly he was hurt. And with that thought in his mind, he passed into unconsciousness.

+++

When Thomes and the others got to where the police had found Val's car, Thomes spoke to one of the police officers. "Have you found anything?" he asked.

"We found a trail of blood, but it looks like he was wandering around in circles, and we can't find a definite trail. We're waiting for the dogs to arrive, but I think we're looking for a body now. Don't you?"

Thomes shook his head. "I don't know. I just don't know. Thank you so much for what you've done."

Thomes went back to his team. "They haven't found him yet, but they're bringing the dogs, so we'll have to wait. Can you remember anything else from last night?" he asked Susanne.

"I don't get this at all," Ricardo said. "First we want him to leave. Then when he goes, we try to find him."

"Oh, shut up! Just because you don't like him …" Susanne said.

"I was just saying. If this is his blood, when and if we find him, it's going to be as a corpse. But at least we're close to the cemetery, so we could just bury him. It'll save time."

"That's it," Thomes said. "*I* remember something! He said he was going to go to Juliet's grave and watch the sun come up. Ricardo, you might just be a genius."

"What are you talking about? And who is Juliet?" Susanne asked.

"There's no time to explain now. Let's go," Thomes said.

"Go? Go where?" Benny asked.

"Into the cemetery," Trena said. "Get an ambulance just in case."

They all set off at a run towards the cemetery. At a run, Thomes, Susanne, and Trena wove off into different directions, between headstones. Finally, Thomes saw a body slumped on a grave. He called to the others as he ran towards it. Thomes turned the body over, and Susanne saw that it was Val. She ran to him with a scream and then fell on her knees crying.

Thomes felt for a pulse. "Yes," he said. "It's weak, but yes."

"The ambulance is on its way," Benny said, huffing and puffing as he joined them.

"No time," Thomes said. "Get the car. We'll take him ourselves. Call the hospital and tell them we're on our way, then cancel the ambulance."

Benny went to get the car. He'd call the hospital once they were underway. The others lifted Val to carry him to the car. As they pick him up, Susanne saw the name Juliet Frankland on the headstone.

The ride to the hospital seemed to take forever. Susanne had got in the backseat, and she had Val's head resting on her knees. She was stroking his hair and talking to him, telling him to hang on, that she loved him, that and they would be at the hospital soon. Her tears fell on his face, and she gently wiped them away.

At last, they arrived at the hospital, and Val was rushed into surgery. After what felt like a lifetime, a doctor came into the waiting room. "Are any of Mr. Frankland's family members here?"

"Yes, me," Thomes said.

Trena stood beside him with her hand on his shoulder. The others stared at Thomes.

"Well, Mr. Frankland—" began the doctor.

"Thomes," he said. "My name is Thomes."

The doctor looked at him: his eyebrows raised. "Well, Mr. Thomes, we have cleaned and dressed his wounds. He is now receiving a blood transfusion. I must say it's a miracle he survived. I have never known anyone to lose so much blood and live. Do you know how he came by these wounds?"

Thomes shook his head. "No, sorry. We just found him in a pool of blood and brought him here. Do you know what made the wounds?"

"I would say it was a long, thin-bladed instrument. We also found a very recent bullet wound that had also started bleeding again. Do you know how he got that?"

"It would seem that my brother is not a popular person."

"So, it would seem," the doctor said.

"How is he?" Thomes asked.

"As I said, his wounds have been cleaned and dressed, and he is receiving blood. In other words, he is stable but unconscious. Plus, he's been sedated."

"Can we see him?" Susanne asked.

"And you are?"

Before Susanne had the chance to answer Thomes said, "She is a close friend and colleague."

"Okay. I suppose you can go in. But, as I said, he's been heavily sedated, so he won't know you're there."

"That's okay," Thomes said. "We'll know."

The doctor summoned a nurse to take them to Val's room, but they were allowed to stay for only a short time.

+++

Thomes and Susanne were sitting quietly in the waiting room. The others had fallen asleep. "I hope he won't be angry with me for being here," Susanne said quietly.

"No," said Thomes. "I told you earlier that, when he said 'it's Ralph', he meant meeting you. Well, he was going to take you out to dinner, tell you about Ralph. Then he was going to ask you to marry him. Then Melanie, Benny, and Ricardo showed up, and he sort of lost it. Most unusual for him. Then when you questioned him about Ralph and what he meant, he evaded the question. When you got angry with him, he did what he does best. He ran."

"How do you know all this?" she asked.

"I've already told you. After he left you he came back to the office, and that's where I found him. And that is how he ended up drunk."

"I thought you didn't like him—didn't want him around," Susanne said.

"Yes, I know what you thought. Now, don't you go blaming Melanie, Ricardo, or Benny? Melanie was trying to push the two of you together, and that is why she appeared where you were last night. She went there to play cupid. You see, she knew as well as I did that Val had fallen for you."

"I can't believe this. Am I the only one who didn't know?"

Thomes laughed. "But you did really. That's why you disobeyed me and went out with him in the first place."

"I didn't know that you and Val were brothers," Susanne said.

"No, I know you didn't."

The nurse came and told them they could see Val again. They all went in and saw Val lying in the bed looking very pale and wasted. Susanne went to him and took his hand; the others gathered around for a few minutes and then left Susanne alone with him.

The doctor came and spoke to Thomes. "I'm sorry," he said. "But I must ask you all to leave now. We will contact you if anything changes."

"Thank you, doctor, but I want to leave Susanne with him until he regains consciousness."

"I'm sorry—" the doctor began. But Thomes held up his hand and stopped him. He took out his official government ID and showed it to the doctor. "Val—Mr. Frankland—is a government agent and a member of my team as well as my brother. Now whoever did this to him might just decide to come back and finish the job. As you have seen, they have already tried twice to kill him, and I don't want to give them a chance to make it third time lucky. So, I want to leave some police officers outside the door to guard him, and I want to leave Susanne, who is also an operative inside the room. When he wakes up, I want him to see a friendly face. Now I know you have procedures to follow, but she must stay with him."

"All right," the doctor said. "I'll have one of the nurses make up a bed for her."

"Thank you very much, doctor. I'll just brief her and the police officers. Then the rest of us will get out of your way."

Thomes went back into the room and told Susanne what was going on. She threw her arms around his neck and hugged him. "Thank you so much."

"You take good care of him."

"I will. Don't worry."

"There are going to be two police officers outside the door just in case. Okay. We'll see you later."

"Okay. I'll call if he wakes up."

Two nurses came in and made a bed up for Susanne. They pushed against the side of Val's bed so she could lie beside him. When the nurses left, Susanne lay beside him, holding his hand, whispering to him, telling him that she loved him, and she would take care of him.

She had a million questions to ask him. Had Val told Thomes how he felt? Or was Thomes just saying that to make her feel better? Maybe he was, and maybe he wasn't. She wouldn't think about that right now. He was alive, and she was with him. That was enough for now.

CHAPTER 9

Juliet's Story

Susanne had not slept the night before, and she couldn't sleep now. She had a nagging feeling that, if she went to sleep, Val would die while she slept. It was foolish, and she knew it, but that didn't change the feeling. The doctor had said that Val was weak but stable. He would recover. It would be slow, but he would recover. Nevertheless, Susanne's feelings persisted. She gave up trying to sleep and pushed the bed out of the way so she could put a chair there. She just sat there still talking to him. She put her head down on his chest and listened to his slow but steady breathing. Before she knew it, she was asleep. She was still like that when Trena came and startled her.

"I'm sorry I didn't mean to make you jump."

"It's okay," Susanne said. She looked at Val.

"Don't worry he'll be fine."

Susanne looked round. "What time is it?"

Trena smiled at her. "You've been asleep most of the day. The nurses have kept looking in on you to make sure you were okay."

Susanne looked surprised. "I've slept all day?"

"Most of it. You must have needed it."

"This is going to sound stupid. I moved the bed and sat in this chair because I had an awful feeling that I was going to lose him if fell asleep."

"It's not stupid at all. He likes you. I can tell you that for certain."

"I thought he did, but then he seemed to change. I wasn't sure what happened. I thought I must have done something wrong."

"As time goes by, you will find that Val hasn't always had an easy time of things, so he tends to try to keep people at arm's length. If you love him, you will have to fight to get close to him. Don't let him push you away. As you've seen, he does try to do that. It's a defense thing with him. He's done it for so long now, I don't think he knows he's doing it, so when you breeched his defenses, he got confused and scared. That is not a normal state for him; that is something I can tell you for sure."

"I tried to ask him about his past, but he just changed the subject," Susanne said.

Trena laughed. "Yes, he would. And that is where you must be persistent. He will answer your questions, but you must keep pushing him. Can you do that?"

"Yes, if I have to," Susanne said.

"Good. It's about time he settled down. He's been running for too long. And I don't want you thinking that you'll push him away. You won't—not if he loves you. And I think he does. By the way, did you know he'd resigned?"

"No, I didn't. He didn't say anything about it. When did he do that?"

"Just before he went out on that last job. He didn't want to say anything until after the job was done and you Sara were safe and sound. He came to see me at home last night to tell me. He said he had found something more important than this job. He said he was going to take you to dinner and tell you that he had quit, and he said he had something to ask you. So, if you're going to stay with him, you will be taking on a lot. He can be very difficult, as you've already seen. You must get him to open up. You must make him talk to you. Don't take no for an answer, and certainly don't let him change the subject. He's going to drive you nuts for a while. Are you up for that?"

"Yes, I can manage that," Susanne said.

"Good." She held out a tote bag she'd been carrying. "Here you go. I thought you might not want to go home, so I brought you a few things."

"Thank you very much. You're right I don't want to leave unless I have to."

"Well, you go to shower and change. I'll sit with him until you get back."

"Thanks." She went to a shower room down the hall, leaving Trena to keep an eye on Val.

Susanne was quick. "Feel better now?" Trena asked when she returned wearing a soft shirt and pants that Trena had brought for her.

"Yes, thanks. I do."

Trena stood and looked down at Val and smiled. "Here, let me take those clothes." She took the bag Susanne held out to her. "I have to go now, but if you need anything, or if anything changes, just call either Thomes or me. Anytime."

"Thank you so much," Susanne said. "But there is one thing before you go. Who is Juliet Frankland?"

Trena looked at her sharply. "Where did you hear that name?"

"When we were looking for Val, both you and Thomes spoke of Juliet. Then we found Val in the cemetery. The name on the headstone was Juliet Frankland. So, I just wondered."

"Juliet was the name of his late wife. I'll ask Thomes or Doc to tell you about her."

Trena left her alone with Val and her thoughts.

+++

Later that evening, Thomes and Benny came to visit. Thomes handed her the now-familiar tote bag. "Here," he said. "Trena asked me to give you this."

"Thank you."

"How is he doing?" Benny asked.

"No change at the moment. But the doctor said he was reducing his sedation, so hopefully, he might wake up soon."

Thomes went to Val's side. He bent down and whispered something in his ear, and then moved away again.

"What was that about?" Susanne asked.

"Oh, nothing. Just saying hello, that's all."

With visiting time over, Thomes and Benny left, leaving Susanne with Val. She went back to sitting beside him until after the lights were out. Then she lay on his bed with him, being careful of all the wires and tubes. She lay there whispering how much she loved him.

The following morning, the nurse came in and suggested that Susanne take a shower while the doctor examined Val and they changed his dressings. "Okay. I'll go get a coffee and have a shower and change."

Susanne got into the shower and just stood there under the water thinking about Val, about how little she knew about him. There were so many questions she wanted to ask, every time she asked a question, not only did people avoid giving her an answer but more questions occurred. She was more confused than ever. As she was thinking about it all, someone knocked on the door.

"Yes?" she asked. "Is everything okay?"

"I think you should come back," the nurse said.

"Why? What's happened? Is everything all right?"

She was sure the nurse was going to say that Val had died while she was showering. But instead, the nurse said, "He's starting to wake up. The doctor is in with him now, but I thought you might want to know."

"Yes, thank you. Thank you very much!" She dried herself and dressed quickly, and then made her way back to Val's room. She had to wait until the doctor had finished his examination. While she waited in the hallway, she called Thomes. He told her they would be there as soon as possible.

When the doctor came out of the room, he smiled at her. "He is doing very well. He will be more out than in for a bit, but he is getting stronger."

"Can I go in now?" Susanne asked.

"Yes, of course. The nurse will be in and out keeping an eye on him until he's fully conscious."

The doctor left, and Susanne went back into Val's room. She looked at him. Did he look slightly different? Maybe a bit more color? She didn't know. Did it matter? *No. If he's all right, that's what matters.* She sat down beside him and took his hand. She put her head on his chest again, listening to the slow, steady beat of his heart and feeling the almost imperceptible rise and fall of his chest as he breathed in and out. She was once again beginning to doze when she felt his hand tighten ever so slightly on hers. Her heart skipped a beat. She sat up and looked at him. "Val? can you hear me?"

He tried to speak. but it came out as a croak.

"What is it? What do you want?"

His eyes fluttered open: he looked at her. "Dry," he croaked.

Susanne called for the nurse. When she came in Susanne said. "Can he have some water, please? He's very thirsty."

"I'm sorry," the nurse said. "He can't have any water just yet. It could make him sick."

"But he needs a drink. He's very dry."

"I'll get some ice cubes," the nurse said. "If you rub one on his lips, that will help. I'll also get the doctor."

When the nurse returned with the ice cubes, Susanne rubbed one of them on Val's lips. He opened his eyes again. His voice still sounded like a croak, but at least it was a bit stronger. He turned his head towards her. "Hello," he said. "And thank you."

"Hello to you as well. How are you feeling?"

"Fine," he said. "But can I have another drink?"

"That was an ice cube. You can't have any waster just yet. It might make you sick, but I suppose I could see give you another one of these ice cubes."

He began to say thanks, but his throat was still very dry, so he just nodded. Susanne took another ice cube from the cup and rubbed it on his lips. He lay back and closed his eyes.

By the time Thomes arrived with Trena, Val was feeling much stronger. Thomes stood beside his bed. "So how are you feeling now?" he asked.

"Hi, Dex. I think I'm wearing the alligator down. It's the tumble dryer and sand that's the problem."

"I've told you not to call me that," Thomes said. "And what are you talking about—alligators, tumble dryers, and sand.?"

"Don't ask me," Val said. "I'm not right in the head."

"Now that is something we agree on," Thomes said.

Melanie and Doc arrived. Melanie sat beside Val and scolded him. "If you ever scare us like that again, I will kick your butt. Do you understand?"

"Yes, Mom, I understand."

Trena asked Susanne how Val was doing.

"He's still weak, but he's doing well. At least that's what the doctor said."

"But what about you? How are you doing?"

"That one's not as easy to answer. I don't know—happy, sad, mixed up, confused. Take your pick."

"Believe it or not, he probably feels the same. Plus, I bet he's still unsure of what happened to him."

Melanie called Susanne. "He wants you," she said.

Susanne went back to his bedside. "Thought maybe you had gone," he said.

"No," she said. "I'll be here for as long as you want me."

"You sure you want to hang around forever?" he said. "It's a long time to hang around with a loser like me."

"Always and forever," she said. "Now it's time for you to rest. I can tell that you're tired."

He looked at Thomes, who had wandered over.

"Just wait until you get better," Trena said.

He smiled and closed his eyes. She was right; he was tired. He had taken his medication, and he was drifting again, but that was okay. He felt safe, happy, at peace.

"Can I ask you something?" Susanne asked Thomes when she was sure Val couldn't hear her.

"You can ask," he said.

"Who was Juliet Frankland?"

Thomes, Trena, and Doc all looked at each other.

"The director said she would ask one of you to tell me," Susanne said.

It was Doc who spoke. "You had better sit down," he said. "We will have to go back a few years to when we first met Val."

"I thought you said you were brothers," she said to Thomes.

"If you will just listen, I will explain it all to you," Doc said, and he led them out of Val's room to a quiet waiting room where they all sat together.

"When Val first came to this country from England with his parents, he was only young, about five years old," Doc began. "He was enrolled in school, and everything was going on quite normally. Then one day—he must have been about seven—his mom and dad dropped him off at school. They were driving across town to visit some friends who had come over from England when an eighteen-wheeler crossed the yellow line and killed them both instantly."

"My God, that's awful," Susanne said.

"Yes, it was," Doc said. "Because now Val was a child alone in a country that was not his birth country, and he had no family to turn to. The local authorities had to try to decide what to do with him. You see, they couldn't send him back to England; he had no family there either. So, the decision was made to foster him out, and he ended up in a series of unfortunate placements. Several families used him as a slave that the families had been paid to take into their homes. Some of the times he was beaten like a bad dog that had piddled on the new carpet. In the last foster home, the father—and I use the term loosely—used to beat Val and quite often leave him without food. The man said it would help to strengthen his character and that it never did him any harm. Then, one day, Val decided that enough was enough, and with the help of a baseball bat, he gave his so-called foster father a good beating. He asked him if his character was any stronger for the beating, and then he ran away. He was twelve at the time, but even at that age, he knew that, if the authorities caught him, they would either put him in an orphanage or another foster home, or even a young offender's institution, so he just kept moving from place to place. I suppose they did look for him, but not very hard. You see, he was a problem that they didn't know what to do with.

Susanne looked at Doc with disbelief.

"You look as though you don't believe a word of what I said," said Doc.

"It's not that I don't believe you," she said. "It's just so awful. That must have gone on for, what, five years? Then they just gave up on him? My god, it's no wonder he doesn't let people near him. Would any of us in the same circumstances?"

"Exactly," Doc said. "Well, he spent the next few months moving around keeping out of sight. Not that anyone was looking for him very hard; he was just another missing kid. He was living rough, sleeping in ditches or anywhere he could find shelter, finding food wherever he could, and going hungry if he couldn't. So, he learned not to trust anyone. Then one night he was feeling a little more tired than usual. He found a barn, crept in, pulled some hay over himself, and fell asleep. And that was where I found him."

Susanne gasped and jumped as if she had been asleep and suddenly been woken up. "You found him?" she said.

"Yes," Doc said. "It was my barn he went to sleep in. He was very ill when I found him—from sleeping rough and not having enough food. He had put out the welcome mat for every kind of bug out there. He had pneumonia plus other assorted medical issues. He was so malnourished, you could count almost every bone in his body. He looked quite pathetic really. He was just lying there shivering. He didn't have the strength to stand up by himself. So I picked him up and carried him into the house, cleaned him up, and put him to bed. Now I have seen a lot of things in my life, but I was disgusted when I saw what they had done to him—the marks on his body from the beatings he had received. He must have gone through hell. But, luckily, I am a doctor, and therefore I didn't have to call in anyone else. I took care of him myself, and I nursed him back to health myself. To this day, I don't know why I didn't tell the authorities that he was with me, but I didn't. He recovered slowly, and once he was better, he asked how he could repay me for what I had done for him. Then he wondered if perhaps I just wanted him to leave. I told him he was more than welcome for any help I had given, but I thought he should stay a little longer just to be sure that he was fully fit. And as for repaying me, there was no need for that, but if he felt that he must, he could help around the place. He said he would quite like to stay a bit longer if he wasn't being too much trouble. I said he was no trouble and that he could stay just as long as he liked. I asked him about going to school. I remember he asked, 'Why would I want to go there?' I could see that trying to argue with him about this would be pointless, so I left it alone. I said that if he wanted me to, I would try to teach him at home the best I could.

"He asked me why I was helping him—being so nice. He asked what was in it for me. I told him there was nothing in it for me. I told him I just liked him for himself. And maybe he reminded me of myself when I was his age.

"He asked if I'd been homeless, useless, and without parents! He was upset. He was doing his best not to cry. I made a point of not noticing. I told him it wasn't like that at all. For one thing, I told him he wasn't useless. I told him he didn't have to be homeless—he could stay there with me. If he didn't want to go to school, I could help him learn at home. When he smiled at me, I felt a bit like crying myself."

"'Home,' he said. He asked how I'd explain him to others if he did stay. I just smiled at him and told him that I'd say he was my sister's son come from England to stay for his health. That got him laughing too. 'You're all right,' he told me. 'At least so far.'

"So, he stayed with me, and I home tutored him for a short while. Eventually, he did go back to school where he made some friends. One of these friends was the son of Lewis and Lilly Thomes, neighbors of mine."

Susanne jumped as if she'd been goosed. "Thomes?"

"Yes," Doc said smiling. "Lewis and Lilly Thomes had two children—a son called Dexter, who was a few years older than Val, and a daughter called Juliet, who was a month younger than Val. It was love-hate at first sight between Val and Juliet. They each said they hated the other, and five years later they were married. She was not unlike you. A little taller maybe. She had darker hair and hazel eyes, but for all the differences, you are very much like her."

Susanne started to speak, but Doc interrupted. "No," he said. "You misunderstand. Val and Juliet were happily married for only a few weeks, but then Juliet died."

"How did she die?" Susanne asked. "Was it some kind of illness?"

"No," Doc said. "Not any kind of illness. She was murdered."

Susanne jumped to her feet. "Murdered? Who? Why?"

"We don't know. That was something we could never figure out. It just didn't make any sense at all. I mean who would want to hurt either of them? They were just a couple of newlywed kids. Val had worked long and hard to save enough money for the deposit on a house, and they were going to look at it. The pair of them were quite excited. I must say I was excited about them. We all were. We watched them get into the car. But Juliet had left the keys on the hall table in my house, so Val got out of the car and was walking up the drive when their car exploded. Val was thrown into the side of my house, and Juliet was, of course, killed instantly. Val was rushed to the hospital where he lay in a coma for about a month. When he woke up, we had to tell him what had happened. Of course, he'd missed Juliet's funeral and everything. We were all quite surprised by his reaction. He took the news very calmly and never said a word. He didn't speak at all for about three months—at least not to any of us. But he began getting into fights. It was after one of these fights when he put three young men in the hospital that he came home and told me he'd joined the army. He packed his clothes and left. After that, we sort of lost touch. We got bits of news about him, but not *from* him—how brave he was, how we could do with more soldiers like him, that sort of thing. You see, he would charge enemy positions on his own or he would go back for others who had been injured, once again on his own. What they saw as selfless bravery we saw as something else."

"You think he was trying to get himself killed," Susanne said.

"Well, that's what we thought. Perhaps *he* thought, if he could get himself killed, he would be with Juliet again," Doc said.

"So you never saw him again until now when he joined the team?"

"Oh, yes, we saw him. With his time served in the army was up, he came here and joined the team."

"You mean here at this agency?"

"Yes, here at this agency. Trena had just been promoted to director, and Thomes had become the team leader. Val was made a senior agent. Melanie and I were doing what we do now. Also, Gary was part of the team, and of course, a young woman who was also called Juliet."

"You have to be joking," Susanne said.

"No joke," Doc said. "Gary was killed by another car bomb—in Val's car. And then Juliet—"

"Don't tell me he married her."

"No, he didn't marry her, but I believe they were … I believe the term is 'an item,' or they were going to become an item."

"So, what happened to her?"

"They went out for a meal, and she was hit by a bullet meant for Val. That's when he left to join another team. I say team, but the agents worked alone. They didn't report into an office as you do. They called in to receive assignments and to report when the tasks were completed. His job was quite simple—hunt down terrorists and neutralize them by whatever means necessary. Now as far we know, he has not made any arrests. At least there are none on record. If there was no doubt they were terrorists, he would terminate them with extreme prejudice, and that was why Val and Thomes fell out."

"My God," Susanne said. "This explains a lot—like why he's so hard to get close to and why he won't talk about his past. It seems to me that he thinks that if he lets himself love others or lets others love him, they will die."

"We think that's it," Doc said. "He has certainly pushed people away for a long time."

"Do you think things might change now?" Susanne said.

Trena, who had been quiet up to now, said, "Well, judging by his reaction to you, plus the fact he has resigned, it might be safe to say that you breached his defenses. And with a little help, he might be ready to try to live again."

Thomes also spoke up. "I want to thank you," he said.

"Thank me? What for?" Susanne asked, sounding surprised.

"For saving his life and bringing him back."

"But I didn't do anything."

"Oh, but you did. If you hadn't come into his life, or if he hadn't found his way into your life, whichever way you prefer it, he would have just carried on the way he was, trying to get himself killed until he succeeded. So, thank you."

"I thought you all hated him so much," Susanne said.

"I know you did. But I think you know a little better now."

Susanne looked at Thomes with tears in her eyes. "I guess I do," she said.

CHAPTER 10

Val Goes Home

When Val woke again, Susanne was beside his bed, and Thomes and Trena were standing just behind her.

"Hi," he said to Susanne. He looked up at Thomes and Trena. "I didn't expect the two of you to be still here."

Trena just looked at him smiling. "Yeah, well I thought that maybe we could start mending a few fences."

"What is it?" he asked. "What's wrong?"

"Nothing wrong," she said. "Nothing's wrong. I'm just happy that you're awake and on the mend. How are you feeling?"

"I don't think I'm quite ready to go out dancing yet but give me an hour. I'm getting there. What happened to me?"

"We were hoping you would be able to tell us that," Thomes said.

"I have no idea," he said. He looked at Thomes. "The last thing I remember is you saying that we should go for a drink." Val looked around the room and began laughing. "You all look as if you're preparing for a funeral," he said.

"You're lucky we're not," Thomes said. "Whoever stuck you did a pretty good job of it. If we hadn't found you when we did ... well, you don't need me to tell you. We'll leave you two alone now. I trust you to behave."

Val grinned. "You're going to leave me alone with a beautiful lady and you want me to behave?"

Thomes laughed. "Okay. We'll see you later."

They both said goodbye and left Susanne and Val alone.

"How long have I been here?" Val asked.

"Only a few days," she said.

"Have you been here all the time?"

"Yes. Well, someone had to make sure you stayed out of mischief."

"And did I stay out of mischief?"

"I think so. But I don't know what you were dreaming about, do I?"

"I want to thank you for being here. I thought, after last time we were together, that you might not want to bother with me anymore."

She squeezed his hand. "You can't get rid of me that easily."

"Good," he said. "Now please tell me what is going on."

"Nothing is going on. Why would you think there is?"

"I don't know. But something is different."

"Well, it could be that, since you wouldn't answer any questions, I had to ask Thomes and Doc about you."

"And did they enlighten you?"

"You could say that. Between them, they told me all about your life from when you were a child until now."

"And you're still here?"

"Don't be angry," she said. "Doc cares about you. So do Thomes and Trena."

"I know. It was Doc who turned my life around. You know, sometimes I think it was more than just luck that I chose Doc's barn. Did he tell you how he found me? Starved almost to death and shivering like a stray dog caught out in a storm."

Susanne struggled to talk. "He told me about what happened to your parents and how, for the next five years, you suffered terribly. I'm not surprised you are the way you are."

"Did he also tell you about Juliet?"

She nodded. "Yes, he told me. Did you ever find out why it happened?"

"I found out that the car I had bought had previously belonged to a local drug dealer. I had three jobs on the go at once. You see, I wanted to be able to give Juliet everything she wanted. If she wanted something, I didn't want to have to say sorry we can't afford that, so I worked and saved until I had the money I needed to put a deposit down on a house she liked. Then I bought a car. As I said, it had belonged to a local drug dealer. It turned out he had been stepping on the wrong people's toes. It seems that someone had decided he was getting too big for his boots and decided that he should be removed from the picture. So, a bomb was planted in his car, but unfortunately, by the time they planted the bomb it had become my car."

She saw the tears running down his face. She wiped them away.

"I hope you're not angry with me for prying."

"No, not at all. I just hope you can forgive me for the way I treated you and for what I am."

"Don't be silly! There's nothing to forgive. It's not as if you had much of a choice. You were forced into being what you are. Anyway, I love you, and that means I forgive everything."

He squeezed her hand again. "So, you're planning on staying then?"

"Of course I am. You're not getting rid of me now!"

"I sure hope not," he said.

"Why didn't you tell me that you had resigned?"

"I had planned to tell you when we went out that night. Then Melanie, Benny, and Ricardo turned up, so I put it off. Then we went back to your place and I got kind of scared and made a total mess of everything."

"So, what are you going to do now?"

"I don't know. I suppose I'll have to look for a job. And then ask you if you might kind of want to wear my ring."

"So, if I say yes, does that mean I get the glamorous lifestyle I was hoping for?"

"I'm not sure. Do you think we could live on love?"

She sighed. "It looks like we might have to. Or I suppose I could keep working and keep us both."

"Hmm … a kept man. I like the sound of that. I always wanted to be a man of leisure."

She shook a fist at him, and he laughed.

"You still look tired. Perhaps you should get some rest."

"Yes, milady. Are you going to go home for a while? You look as if you could use some rest yourself."

"I don't know. Maybe I should stay here with you."

"You go home. It'll be okay. I'll be okay. And I'll still be here when you get back."

She bent over and kissed him. When she left the room, he was alone with his thoughts. Was he being fair to Susanne? He knew that he loved her, and she had said she loved him, but look at what had happened to everyone else he had loved. He thought he would talk to her again and explain how unsure he felt. He would tell her what had happened to everyone he had ever loved. He thought he knew the answer to that, but he had to try. With those thoughts in his head, he fell asleep.

When Val opened his eyes, he was surprised that Susanne was sitting beside him. "Hi," he said. "I thought you were going home for a while."

"And good morning to you. I did go home last evening, and I came back this morning, sleepyhead."

Val looked at her with his mouth open.

"Close your mouth before you start to catch flies," she said. "You must have needed your sleep. I must say you look better for it."

"Are you saying I looked a bit rough?"

"Just a little bit," she said, smiling.

"Be careful what you say, or I might have to smack your bottom."

She stood and looked at him. "You shouldn't promise what you can't deliver," she said. "Anyway, we don't have time. The others have come to see you if you're up for that."

He smiled. "Yeah, I feel good today."

"There is just one thing."

"And, pray tell, what is that?"

"Lewis has come to see you. If you want to see him, that is."

The smile faded off Val's face.

"I'm sorry," she said. "It's just that I thought it might be okay. So you could put it all behind you. I know you haven't seen him since just after Juliet died, but he was your father-in-law, and I thought you might want to put all that behind you."

"I guess you're right," he said. "Perhaps it has been in the way for too long."

They all entered Val's room. Thomes stood back as Lewis approached Val's bed.

"Hello Val," Lewis said. "It's been a long time."

"Yes, it has," Val replied. "How have you and Lilly been keeping?"

"Not bad, you know. What about you?" Lewis asked.

"Oh, you know how it is—no rest for the wicked, so they say."

"Look," Lewis said. "I came here to see you and make sure you're all right, but also to say that we—Lilly and I, that is—are sorry for the things we said after Juliet died. We know it wasn't your fault."

"It's taken you all these years to figure that out?" Val said.

"No, it hasn't, and we've tried to get in touch with you throughout the years, but you would never take or return our calls. We tried leaving messages. I even tried writing to you, but we never got any response at all. I can understand that you would be angry with us for the things we said. We have tried our best to apologize, but it has taken something awful like this for me to get the chance."

Val just looked at him; he didn't speak. The silence in the room was tangible. Susanne was watching Val, silently praying for him to say something—anything—but still, Val didn't speak.

Eventually, Lewis said. "Well, I hope you get better real soon. And we are sorry. It was just that we were hurting, and we didn't know how to deal with it. So we turned on the only person we could—you." Lewis turned and started for the door. "I'll tell Lilly you're doing well. She still asks about you every day."

Val spoke just as Lewis's hand gripped the door handle. "Lewis, please … wait. Where's Lilly?"

Lewis turned and looked back at Val. "She's at home. She didn't come just in case you refused to speak to us or to even see us. She couldn't take that. She has always loved you like a son. She always kept up with what you were doing—as much as she could anyway. She kept everything the army sent us. She still shows them off to anyone willing to look. Maybe you could find the time to come visit when you get out of here and feel up to it. Welcome back."

"Thank you," Val said. "But it's not me you should thank. It's Susanne. Without her, I don't think I would even be here. As soon as I get out of the hospital, I will come and visit. I promise."

"Maybe Susanne would like to come as well," suggested Lewis.

"What do you think?" Val asked Susanne.

"Of course! I would love to," she said. "Besides I'm not letting you go off without me."

The mood in the room had lightened, and everyone but Ricardo began to chat. He announced to no one in particular that he had a prior engagement, and he left. At one point, a nurse popped her head in the door to ask them to keep the noise down a bit.

"So how long do you think you'll be in here?" Lewis asked.

"I'm hoping they're going to let me out in a couple of days."

"Have you got anything planned?"

"No," Val said. "Just rest under the watchful eyes of 'Nurse Susanne'."

Susanne stuck her tongue out at him.

"If you come over to us you can stay as long as you like," said Lewis. "As you know, it's quiet and peaceful—just the place for rest and recuperation."

"Sounds perfect," Susanne said.

"That's settled then," said Val. "As soon as they let me go, we'll come over. Maybe we could have a party?"

"No parties," Susanne said. "You have to rest."

Val looked at Lewis for help. But he just smiled. "Looks like you might have met your match— again," he said with a chuckle.

Finally, everyone said their goodbyes and left Susanne and Val together. "Lewis seems very nice," she said. "But for a moment there, I thought you were going to just let him walk away. I thought you weren't going to say anything."

"Yeah, I know. It was hard for them when Juliet died. They thought that, if she hadn't met and married me, she would still be alive. Maybe she would be. Maybe it was my fault."

"Stop right there," she said. "That's enough. It wasn't your fault. I know I wasn't there, but I know you. You wouldn't have knowingly let something like that happen." He looked at her. "I just know," she said. "No more arguments."

"Do you know that I love you?" he asked.

"Well, I was beginning to wonder," she said, smiling.

"When they let me out of here, it will be good to go see Lewis and Lilly. You'll like Lilly. She's a darling. She might even try to adopt you."

"That would nice. It sounds like something to look forward to."

They decided it would be best if Susanne went home again and got some rest. She kissed him goodnight and went home.

As Val lay in bed thinking about Susanne and drifting towards sleep, he sensed someone in the room. His instincts told him something wasn't right. He opened his eyes a fraction at first, thinking it may be a nurse. Even though he couldn't see whomever it was clear, he could see that the figure was a man, and he was wearing a hoodie. Val lay still not wanting the man to suspect that he was awake. Val watched the man inject something into his IV. He lay still. As soon as the man had left the room, he immediately folded the IV tubing so nothing could flow through it. Then he called for the nurse. When the nurse came in, Val told her what had happened, but she didn't believe him. He insisted that she change his IV.

"Calm down, Mr. Frankland," she said. "You've probably just had a bad dream. No one has been in here. Now please let go of this tubing."

"No!" Val said. "Someone was in here. He injected something into my IV line. You need to change it. Now!"

"Mr. Frankland, please be sensible let go of the tubing."

Val shook his head. "Not until you change it."

The nurse placed a call to Val's doctor, Dr. Gee, and told him what was happening. The doctor said he was on his way. He asked the nurse to call Susanne while he called Thomes.

When Dr. Gee arrived in Val's room, he asked Val what the problem was. Still holding onto the crimped tubing, Val explained what had happened and said that he wanted his IV changed. The doctor sighed.

"Okay, Mr. Frankland, we'll change your IV." He turned to the nurse. "Nurse, will you change this IV for me? I want this one sent to the laboratory for testing, just to be sure."

The nurse removed Val's IV and replaced it with a fresh one.

+++

Susanne was getting out of the shower when Val's phone rang. She recognized her number and smiled: it was Val. He was probably calling to say goodnight.

She answered the phone. "What are you doing?" she asked. "You should be resting."

"Miss Wilder." She didn't recognize the strange voice.

"Yes, that's me. Who are you? And what are you doing with this phone?"

"Miss Wilder, this is Nurse Harrison. I'm taking care of Mr. Frankland. We need you to come to the hospital as soon as you can."

"Why? What's happened?"

"We are having a problem with Mr. Frankland. We think he had a bad dream, and now he's becoming hysterical. He thinks someone is trying to kill him."

"I'm on my way. I'll just call Agent Thomes and then I'll be there."

"There's no need to call Agent Thomes. Dr. Gee is doing that now."

"Thank you," Susanne said. "I'll be there as soon as I can.

She got dressed as fast as she could. As she was getting ready, she thought about what the nurse had said. She couldn't imagine that. The thought of Val becoming hysterical didn't seem possible.

+++

Thomes sat at his desk in his study. He called it his study, but it was more of a closet that was just big enough for his desk and a single filing cabinet. Various awards were hanging on the wall. There was also a photo of Thomes with Trena, Val, and Doc, and Thomes was looking at it when his phone rang. "Hello," he said.

"Agent Thomes? This is Doctor Gee. The nurse on duty just called to say she is having a problem with Mr. Frankland."

"What kind of problem?" Thomes asked. He was suddenly on high alert.

"She said he had a bad dream and woke up saying that someone was trying to kill him. The nurse is most distressed."

"I'm on my way," Thomes said. He got in his car and headed for the hospital. By the time he got there, Susanne was already there. They waited in the hallway while Dr. Gee checked Val's vital signs. When he came out of the room, it was Thomes who spoke to him. "What happened?" he asked.

"Your brother was insistent that someone has tried to kill him. He said that someone injected something into his IV."

"What?" Thomes said. "How the hell did that happen? There were two police officers stationed outside his room. How did anyone get into his room?"

"I asked the nurse about that," Dr. Gee said. "I was told that the officers had been called away to deal with an emergency."

"What?" Thomes almost shouted. "Okay. Never mind about that right now. Please tell me how Val is."

"He is unconscious right now. It seems that someone did indeed enter his room and inject a substance into his IV. Luckily, because he acted so quickly, he received only a very small amount of whatever it was. But he got enough to make him very ill. I don't suppose you would care to tell me what is going on, Mr. Thomes?"

"Sorry, but I can't do that. But I need to know if he can be moved."

"I would strongly advise against that."

"How long before he can be moved?" Thomes asked.

"I don't know, two weeks? It's difficult to say."

"I'm sorry," Thomes said. "We have to move him now."

"I've already told you that we can't. If you move him now, you could kill him."

"Well we can't just leave him here for whoever did this to try again, can we?"

"I'm afraid I still have to say no."

"Okay, thank you, doctor … I'm sorry I don't know your name."

"I am Doctor Gee."

"Thank you, Dr. Gee. I will discuss what we should do next with the other members of my team."

The doctor left them and went to see his other patients.

Thomes had called Trena on his way, and she arrived with the rest of the team. Thomes told them everything that had happened. "The doctor says that, if we move him, we could kill him," Thomes said.

"So, what are we going to do?" Susanne asked.

"I have an idea," said Thomes, "but I'll have to talk to the doctor first." I've asked to see him when he has a moment."

"What do you have in mind?" Trena asked him.

"I would rather wait until Dr. Gee gets here. I don't want to have to go through it twice." Thomes said.

No one spoke much while they waited. Eventually, Dr. Gee came back. "I'm sorry I took so long, but I have to take care of my other patients."

"Yes, of course," Thomes said. "Look, I know you want to keep Val here, but it's like I said—we need to get him out of here. I can assure you he will be in safe hands. We have our doctor. You might have heard of him—Dr. Donald Sibbald."

"Yes, of course, I know Dr. Sibbald. We have met on many occasions."

"That is who will be taking care of him. And we have our facility."

"What do you have in mind?" Dr. Gee asked.

"I would like to tell everyone that this attempt on Val's life was successful—that Val is dead. As he is still unconscious, we could just wheel him out in a body bag, and no one would know the truth but us."

"I don't like this," said Dr. Gee. "I don't like it at all. If I agree to this, it means having to falsify documents. I would have to issue a death certificate."

"I know, and I understand. But If we leave him here—alive—we might as well paint a bullseye on his chest. This way maybe we can take the pressure off a bit."

It took a little time and a lot of persuasions to get Dr. Gee to agree, but finally, he did.

"Thank you so much for this," Thomes said. "Now, whoever did this could be watching the hospital, and if they know for certain that Val is alive, they will come after him again. So, what I propose is that, if the doctor agrees, we put Val in a body bag and take him back to our office to Doc's room."

"But what if he wakes up while he's in the bag?" Susanne asked.

"What do you think, Dr. Gee, can you make sure he stays asleep?" Thomes asked.

"That's no problem, but I still think it's a bad idea to move him."

Susanne went back to Val's bedside and looked at him. Val's eyes fluttered open. "Hello there," she said. She was crying.

"I hope you're not going to be a crybaby when we're married," he said

"Married?" she said, sounding surprised.

"Yes. Sorry, did I forget to mention that?"

"And just what makes you think I would marry you?"

"Because you love me."

"Oh yeah? And who told you that?"

"Why you did. And, besides, I love you, so you have to marry me to make an honest man of me."

"Now you're making fun of me," she said.

"No, I would never make fun of you."

"Are you serious?" she asked.

"Of course I am. That is if you want to. If you do, then you're stuck with me."

She was still crying, but this time her tears were tears of joy.

"I love you so very much," she said

CHAPTER 11

Death Comes Calling

Susanne was sitting beside Val holding his hand. She was talking to him, trying to explain what was going on.

"I know what Thomes wants," Val said. "He needs me to be dead for a while."

"But you won't be dead," she said, sounding a little concerned.

"I know. But I think Dexter is right. I have to die—or at least appear to die for a while. Otherwise, they—whomever they are—will keep coming back until they succeed and finish the job of killing me for real."

"The doctor said he could give you something to make you seem as if you're dead."

"There's no need for that. I can slow down my bodily functions until it seems like I'm dead."

"What do you have to do?" Susanne asked him.

"Normally I do it on my own, but this time I will ask the doctor to give me a sedative to speed the process up. Then I will do the rest."

Doctor Gee came to his bedside. "Are you sure you want to do this?" he asked Val.

Val nodded. "I'm ready."

After Dr. Gee asked everyone to leave the room, he called the nurse and asked her to bring him the drug he needed. When he had it in hand, he filled a syringe and again asked Val if he was certain about what they were about to do. Val nodded, so Dr. Gee injected Val with the contents of the syringe. "It will take a few moments for the drug to work," he told Val. "Would you like your friends to come back in?"

Val nodded. Thomes and the rest of the team came back in. Susanne went to Val's bedside. She could see that whatever the doctor had given him was beginning to work. "Are you okay?" she asked him.

The others had gathered around Val's bed.

"I'm good," Val said. "Feel light and sleepy. I'll see you on the other side."

"If we're spared," Melanie finished for him.

Val smiled, and his eyes closed.

"So, what happens now?" Susanne asked.

"Now we wait," Thomes said.

They all stood around and watched Val and the monitors that he was still attached to. They watched Val's heart rate begin to drop and his respiration slow down. The alarms on the machines began to sound. Dr. Gee moved forward, but Thomes grabbed his arm to stop him.

"No, wait," Thomes said. "It's okay. This is normal."

"Normal? What do you mean normal? He's going into cardiac arrest! We have to help him." Dr. Gee said.

"No," Thomes said. "It's a little trick he uses sometimes. If you check very, very carefully, you might detect a heartbeat, but I doubt it. So now, if I can trouble you for the paperwork, we will get out of your hair."

"I still think this is a bad idea," said Dr. Gee. "And issuing a death certificate for someone who isn't dead is highly illegal."

"I know, but it's for a good cause—saving Val's life."

Dr. Gee finally gave in and issued the necessary paperwork.

Thomes and the team members put Val in a body bag and wheeled him out to their van and drove back to their office. When they arrived at the loading area, they wheeled Val, still in a body bag, out of the back of the van. They wheeled him directly to Doc's medical room, which was laid out like a mini-hospital ward. Once they were safely inside, they unzipped the body bag and transferred Val to one of the beds.

"When are you going to wake him up?" Susanne asked.

"We don't wake him up," Thomes said. "He does that on his own. Doc will give him a shot of adrenaline to get him going, like a bit of a boost. So, as soon as Doc is ready, we can start—"

"Right," Doc said, wheeling a cart containing medical equipment to the bedside. "First things first. We need to connect him to the heart rate and respiration monitor so we can keep an eye on his vital signs. Let's get some blankets ready. He might feel a bit cold."

Benny fetched blankets while Doc connected Val to the monitor. "Right. Here we go," Doc said. He gave Val an injection of adrenaline.

"Will it take long to work?" Susanne asked.

"It should start to work in a few minutes. But be ready. He could feel disoriented and a bit sick."

They all stood around and waited.

"It's taking too long," Susanne said. "It's been at least ten minutes."

Doc examined Val. "Nothing," he said. "No vital signs at all. I told you this was risky. I knew it was a bad idea."

"Can't you give him another injection?" Benny asked. "You know—to give him more of a jump start?"

"No," Doc said. "It wouldn't do any good to give him more. I'm sorry, but it looks like he's gone. It seems that we—should I say I— have managed to do what they—whomever they are—have been trying so hard to do. I've managed to kill my son."

Susanne sat beside Val holding his hand.

"Wake up!" she said. "You have to wake up. You promised. You said we would get married. You can't leave me alone after you promised! You have to come back."

Melanie put her arms around Susanne. They were both crying. "Come on," she said. "It's over. He's gone."

"No!" Susanne screamed. She turned to Thomes. "This is all your fault! You did this and now he's dead. You killed your brother. I hate you!"

"Susanne," he said. "I'm so sorry."

"Sorry!" she shouted. "Sorry? He's dead because of you, and you just say, 'Oh, sorry. Let's get on with something else'?"

"It's not like that," Thomes said. He might have said more, but just then the monitor beeped.

"Hey—that was the monitor," Benny said.

There was another beep, and then another. Susanne went back to Val's side and took his hand. "Yes," she said. "That's it—come back!"

As she watched, his chest began to rise and fall as he began to breathe.

"Yes!" Susanne cried. "That's it! Come on! Come back to me!"

"Get the oxygen!" Doc shouted.

Slowly, Val came back. He was only semiconscious. He looked pale, drawn, and badly used. Susanne, still holding his hand, put her head down on his chest and cried. She felt his hand on her head. She reached up, took his hand in hers, put it to her lips, and kissed it.

"I thought I told you not to be a crybaby," he said. His voice was weak, but at least he was alive.

She looked up. He was smiling, and she smothered his face with kisses. "You're back! You're alive!" she said.

"I sure hope so," he said. "But I think I'm getting too old for this shit."

"How do you feel?" Doc asked him.

"I feel like I've been wrestling an alligator and then sleeping in a tumble dryer."

Thomes came to his bedside and looked at him. "If you ever scare me like that again, I'll kill you myself," he said.

"Sorry, Dex," Val said.

"I've told you not to call me that," Thomes said.

The others gathered around. Susanne and Melanie were still weeping. Ricardo stood back apart from the group.

"I want to say I'm sorry for what I put you through," Thomes said. But I had to make people believe that you're dead."

Susanne turned to Thomes. "I want to apologize for the things I said," she said. "I was just angry."

"I understand," Thomes said. "But let's not dwell on it. What's past is past. You know, I was just thinking that the two of you could do with a holiday."

"A holiday?" Val said. "Now there's a thought. That sounds like something I could go for. I don't suppose you know a good travel agent, do you?"

"As a matter fact I do," Thomes said smiling. "Since mom and dad would like you to go visit for a while, I was thinking that, right after your funeral, you should go and stay there until we can find who's trying to kill you."

"That sounds like a plan to me," Val said.

"I was going to suggest that you go now, and Susanne follow after the funeral, but I don't know if I could stand the arguments."

"Wise man," Susanne said.

"The thing is," Doc said, "what do we do with him until then? I mean he can't live here, can he?"

"He'll come home with me," Susanne said. "I can take some time off for bereavement, and I'll take care of him."

"Okay, that's that problem solved," Thomes said.

"No," Val said.

"No? What do you mean no?" Susanne asked.

"Look, anyone watching to make sure that I am dead would watch your place. He—or she—would probably have the whole team watched just to be sure."

How do you know that?" Susanne asked.

"Because it's what I would do."

"I think he's right," Thomes said. "We have to get him out of town for now, somewhere quiet and isolated. Ricardo, I want you to start looking for somewhere Val can go for now."

"Right. I'm on it," Ricardo said, but he didn't look happy about it.

Val took Susanne's hand. "This is for the best. I know you would like me to be with you at your place, and I would love to be there. But we have to make whoever is trying to kill me think they have succeeded and that I'm dead."

"I know," she said. "I'll come and see you if I can."

"Just for once, I would very much like to get out of this alive," Val said.

Thomes and Trena looked at each other and smiled. Trena looked at Val and said, "Welcome home."

Val looked at her puzzled. "What do you mean?"

"Think about it," Thomes said.

Unless they meant him waking up from that last episode he couldn't think of anything else. "I have no idea what you're on about. But then that's nothing new."

"That's okay," Trena said. "We do."

Val shrugged and smiled. "As long as someone does."

"All right, let's think about arrangements for moving Val," Thomes said.

+++

The funeral for Val was arranged for the following week and went off without a hitch. A lot of people attended, and most of them spoke to Thomes and Trena to say how sorry they were. Many of them were introduced to Susanne, and they told her how sorry they were for her loss. Susanne looked around at all the people there. It didn't seem right to let these people think that Val was dead. But it was as Thomes had said—better to let people think he was dead than for him to be dead.

After the service was over, Thomes spoke to Susanne. He gave her his parents' address and told her that she should wait for a few days and then go there. He told her that Val would join her a few days after that, once they had made sure it was safe.

Susanne had approved of Thomes's plan. She went home and made herself a cup of tea and thought about Val. It seemed to her that she had thought about nothing else since he had appeared—a mystery man with a dark past. But, hopefully, he had a bright future, and she was going to be part of that future. She had about a million questions to ask, but would she get any answers? Maybe not. Maybe some questions were better left unanswered. She thought about how Thomes's and the director's attitudes had changed towards him. At first, it seemed that they hated him and wanted him gone, but now they were doing all they could to protect him. It seemed that everyone liked Val except Ricardo; he was the only one who hadn't seemed to warm to Val, but she put it down to jealousy and a clash of personalities. Soon enough she would know how wrong she was; she would find out just how much Ricardo hated Val.

Two days after the funeral, Susanne loaded up her car and drove to Lewis and Lilly's house. It wasn't a long drive, and when she turned into the yard and stopped, Lewis came out to meet her. *He must have been watching for me*, she thought. When she got out of the car, he hugged her. Welcome," he said. "We've been looking forward to your arrival."

"It's good to be here," she said. "Where's Lilly?"

"Oh, she's inside waiting," he said. "Come on. Let's go inside. I'll get your bags in a while. Right now, come and meet Lilly." He took her arm and almost dragged her into the house.

An elegant-looking, white-haired woman of middle height came forward to meet her. "Hello," she said. "I'm Lilly, and you must be Susanne. I've heard so much about you. It's so good to meet you at last."

As the two women hugged a familiar voice behind her said. "Don't I get one of those?" She turned around so fast she almost fell over. There, sitting in a wheelchair, was Val. She went to him and gave him a hug and a kiss. "Now that's what I'm talking about," he said.

"What are you doing here?" she asked.

"Are you disappointed?" Val asked.

"You know I'm not! But I thought you were coming down in a couple of days when it was safe."

"I was supposed to, but I couldn't wait, so I rang Lewis and asked him to come and get me. And here I am."

"You could have let me know."

"What, and spoil the surprise?"

Over the next few weeks, Thomes came to visit fairly regularly to see how Val was doing. For Susanne, the weeks at Lewis and Lilly's house were like heaven, but they passed so quickly. Val was well on his way back to full fitness. He was working out and taking long walks with Susanne. She felt that she was the happiest person on earth.

+++

When the morning came when Susanne had planned to return to work, she didn't want to go. Val and Susanne were sitting on the porch when Val said it was time for her to go back home. "Why can't I stay here with you?" she asked.

"Because it's time for you to go home and get back to work. I will follow in a few weeks." She stood and looked at him with her hands on her hips. "If you don't go back to work," he reasoned, "how am I ever going to become a kept man?" Susanne started laughing. "That's better," he said. He took her hands and looked into her eyes. "I just need a little time," he said. "I can't just reappear, can I? Everyone thinks I'm dead. Remember?"

"Yes, I know that. So how long before you can come home?"

"I need to find who wants me dead. Then I can see about making a plan for coming home. Thomes and the rest of the guys are doing their best to find who it is. Normally I would just find them myself, but they seem to one step ahead of me all the way."

"How are we going to tell people that you're alive after we've held a funeral for you?"

Val laughed, "Yeah, I know. It's going to be weird: Val Frankland does his Jesus impression and rises from the dead! We'll have to think about that when the time comes. If I just reappear, people will freak out. We'll have to tell people what happened and that I had to drop out of sight for a while."

"So, what are you going to do while you wait?" Susanne asked him.

"I think now is a good time to lay my past to rest. If I don't do it now, it will haunt me forever. As it is, I have been carrying it for long enough."

"You mean Juliet?" she said.

"Yes. I have been carrying that situation with me for too long." He tapped his head with his forefinger. "In here. And now it's time to put it down, to find somewhere comfortable for it to stay. I have carried it long enough. If I don't do it now, I never will, and I want to give us a chance without this in the way." Susanne just looked at him without speaking. "I love you," he said. "And you love me, don't you?"

"Yes, of course, I do. You know I do."

"Then please do as I ask."

"Okay," she said. "But if you don't come soon, then I'm going to come back and get you."

"Fair enough," he said.

"Do you remember what you said to me when you woke up in the hospital when I was sitting by your bed?" Susanne asked.

"Yes, of course. I said I hoped you weren't going to be a crybaby when we were married. Why?"

How did you know that I would marry you?"

"I didn't. I just hoped that either, A, you wanted to marry me or, B, I could surprise you into saying yes!"

She looked at him trying to figure out if he was joking or not. He took her into his arms and kissed her. "Okay," she said, "I'll go back. But I meant what I said—if you don't come back, I will come and get you."

"That sounds good to me," he said.

Val watched Susanne get into her car and drive away. When she was lost to sight, he walked back to the house.

+++

Susanne drove home still thinking about what life was going to be like with Val. She had spent a few weeks with him, and she was so happy. Soon she would be his wife, and they would be together forever. She thought she would speak to Thomes to see if he could find Val a job within the agency. Once she got home, she called Val to let him know she was home safe. They chatted for a while and then said good-bye. She rang Melanie to let her know she was home.

"That's great!" Melanie said. "So how did it go?"

"It went well. We had a great time."

"Is Val back with you?"

"No, he's staying there for another few weeks. We have to figure out how to tell all the people who attended his funeral that he's still alive. But he did ask me to marry him."

"He asked you to marry him?" Melanie shouted.

"Well maybe *asked* is a bit of an exaggeration. He just sort of said 'when we're married', and I thought that might be as close as he actually would ever get to ever asking me."

"So, what did you say?"

"I said I would think about it."

"You didn't!" Melanie said.

"Of course I did. So I thought for about half a second and then said yes."

"This is just so exciting! Have you told anyone else yet?"

"No, not yet. Just you. I'll tell the others later. Val said I should call you and tell you it's Ralph."

Melanie laughed. "This is just so cool."

"And, also, I wanted to ask you if you would be my maid of honor?"

"Of course I will! Thank you!"

"Do you think that Thomes might give Val a job? When he gets back?"

"Don't say anything, but I think the director is going to offer him a job."

"I don't suppose you know what sort of job?" Susanne asked.

"I'm not sure, but I think it has something to do with training."

"That would be amazing."

They talked for a little longer about other things and then hung up. That night, Susanne went to bed thinking that things were going to work out all right. Or so she thought then.

CHAPTER 12

The Road Home

Val was sitting on the porch at Lewis and Lilly's house thinking about how things had changed over the past few weeks, and how Susanne had been responsible for just about all of those changes. He found himself thinking about his birth parents—what he could remember about them. He wished they could have met Susanne; he was sure they would have loved her just as much as he did. He thought that even Juliet would approve and that she would tell him their relationship was all right with her.

After Juliet died, he thought that he would never let himself love anyone ever again. But then he had met Susanne. She had smiled at him, and that had been it. He had been lost. As soon as they found and dealt with whomever it was who was trying to kill him, he would marry Susanne. Then, he supposed, he would have to find a job. He smiled to himself. What kind of job could he do? This was something he had never considered before. He didn't think there would be many jobs in the wanted section for someone good at killing people. Still, there must be something he could do. His thoughts were interrupted when a car pulled into the yard. When it stopped, a man got out and walked towards Val. "Can I help you?" Val asked.

"Maybe you can," the man said. "I'm looking for a Valentine Frankland."

"Then I'm afraid you're out of luck," Val said. "There's no one here by that name."

"I was asked to deliver a letter to him at this address," the man said.

"I've already told you there's no one here by that name," Val said.

"Well, maybe I could just leave it here with you, in case he turns up," the man said, holding it out to him. Val looked at the man and then at the envelope, but he didn't try to take it. "Who is it from?" Val asked.

"I don't know," the man said. "I was given this letter and an envelope full of cash and asked to deliver this envelope to this address. So here I am."

"Yes, here you are," Val said.

The man held out the letter again.

Val reached out and took the letter. "Thank you."

"You're welcome," the man said. "You have a nice day." The man got back in his car and drove away.

Val was just sitting there looking at the letter in his hand when Lilly came out of the house. "Who was that?" she asked.

"Oh, it was just someone from the local office delivering me a letter."

"Susanne is such a sweet girl and I'm not trying to pry into your affairs. But I thought I heard the two of you talking about marriage."

"Yes, I've asked Susanne to marry me, and she has agreed."

"Oh, that is so wonderful," she said. "I am so happy for both of you. You have been alone for far too long. Lewis and I have been hoping that you would find someone. I know you loved Juliet, and I hope you don't mind me saying this, but I think it's time to let her go and move on."

Val stood and hugged Lilly. "Yes, you're right. I think it's time."

Lilly smiled at him. "Plus, Lewis and I were thinking it would be nice to have some grandchildren to spoil. We're not getting any younger, and it doesn't look as if Dexter is going to make us grandparents any time soon."

Val laughed. "Yeah, I think it would be kind of nice to have kids. I don't know what sort of father I'd make."

"You would make a wonderful father."

"Thanks. You know, I was wondering if you and Lewis would act as Susanne's parents. She was an only child, and both of her parents are dead."

"Oh, my, yes we would be so happy to do that. She does look quite a bit like Juliet, so it would be like having her back again."

He hugged her again. She saw the tears in his eyes and wiped them away for him.

"I'm just going for a walk," he said. "Try to clear my head."

"Okay. Will you be leaving soon?" she asked.

"Yes," he said. "If I don't, Susanne will come and drag me back." He laughed.

"Well, you be careful," she said and kissed his cheek.

"I will. I promise."

As Val walked, he opened the envelope and took out a single sheet of paper. He read the message:

Dear Val,

Forgive me for not delivering this to you in person, but as I am sure you will understand, circumstances dictate that I should not. We have your girlfriend as our guest, and we would like to extend an invitation to you to join us. If you decide to accept, simply call the number at the bottom of this letter, and we will release her unharmed. However, if you decide to decline our offer, then we may have to discuss things with her in your stead. We await your call to give us your answer.

Yours,

Royce

Val's old nemesis, Royce Lyme—aka Luciano—had added a phone number at the bottom of the page. Val stood with the letter in his hand. He screamed out loud. He was shaking with rage. They had found him, but now it was Susanne who was in danger. He decided there was only one way to handle the situation—first he would make sure that Susanne was safe. Then he would take care of these people his way. He had tried the "play nice" approach, which is what Thomes had wanted, and it hadn't worked. So now he would use all of his skills—everything he had ever learned—and anyone who got in his way was going to die. They had just made a very big mistake: they had made it personal. Now there was nothing on this earth that was going to stop him. He would see this finished, but his way.

He called Susanne's number but got no answer, so he called Melanie.

"Hi there, and what can I do for you today?" she said.

"Hi. Look have you seen Susanne today?"

"No, not today. Not yet anyway. Not getting cold feet, are you?"

"So she told you, did she?"

"Yes, and she is so excited you know."

"Yeah, so am I—and just a little scared."

"Is something wrong?" Melanie sounded worried.

"No, nothing's wrong. It's just that I was going to stay here for a bit longer, but I've decided to come back. That's all. I was just going to tell her, but she doesn't seem to be at home. If you see her, will you ask her to call me?"

"Are you sure nothing's wrong?" Melanie asked.

"Yes, I'm sure. Everything's good."

"Well if you're sure."

"Yes, I'm sure. Look, I've got to go. I'll see you when I get back."

"Okay then. Bye."

"Bye," he said, and he hung up.

+++

Melanie looked at her phone. *Something isn't right*, she thought. No matter what Val had said, something was wrong. She just felt it. She would talk to Thomes to see what he thought. If he felt the same way, he would know what to do.

When she told Thomes about her conversation with Val and how she felt something didn't feel right—how he sounded off—he said, "He might just have premarital jitters, but I'll talk to him if that makes you feel better."

Thomes tried to call Val's mobile but got no answer, so he called his parents' phone. It was his mother who answered the phone. "It's so nice to hear from you," she said. "And to what do we owe the honor of this call?"

"Is Val there?" he asked.

"No, he's not here. He got a letter this morning, but the man who delivered it wasn't a mailman. I did ask him about it. He said it

131

was from the local office. I thought it might have been from Susanne. He said he was going for a walk, and I haven't seen him since then. Is something wrong?"

"No," Thomes said. "But as soon as he gets back, ask him to call me right away, will you?"

"Okay, I will. Are you sure that everything's all right?" she asked again.

"Yes," he said. "It's just that Susanne is missing him. You know how it is."

"Yes, I know," she said. "If you're sure there's nothing else … bye for now."

"Yeah, bye, Mom. Talk to you later. Give my love to Dad."

Melanie was looking at Thomes. "You look worried," she said.

"I am," he said. "First Susanne hasn't come to work and hasn't called in. And there's no answer when we try to call her cell or home phone. Then Val gets a letter delivered by hand—a letter he said came from the local office—and then he just disappears and doesn't answer his phone."

"Local office?" Melanie said. "We *are* the local office."

"I know that," Thomes said. "And that's what worries me." He walked to his office door. "Benny, get over to Susanne's place and see if she's there. If she isn't … well, you know what to do."

"On my way, boss."

"Ricardo, I want you to go to my parents' house. Have a look around. Keep it low profile. I don't want them to know you're there. Okay?"

"Okay, boss. I'm on it."

"We need to find them," Thomes said. He looked at Melanie. "I think you're right. Something is way off here, and I don't like it."

+++

Val punched in the contact number that was at the bottom of the letter.

"Hello?" It was an unfamiliar male voice.

"This is Val. I was given this number."

"Okay. Have you got a pen and paper."

"I've got a memory," Val said.

The voice grunted and said. "Okay then remember this address then disable your phone. Go to the address I just gave you. You'll find another cell phone there. Call on that phone, and we'll talk." The line went dead. Val looked at his phone. Then he threw it off into the woods.

+++

When Benny got back from Susanne's he said, "She's not there, so I asked around. One of her neighbors said she saw Susanne this morning. She said that she saw her leave for work as usual. She hadn't seen her since."

"Can you trace her phone?" Thomes asked. "And Val's?"

"Sure, no problem—if they're turned on."

"Then why are you still standing here?"

"Sorry, boss." Benny went to his computer and started a search. After a few minutes, he said, "I've got them! Susanne is close to her home, and Val's is near your parents' house. Both phones are on, but they're not moving."

"Call Ricardo. See if he's found anything. If he hasn't, tell him to get back here. And while you're at it, put out a BOLO on both Susanne and Val."

"Doing that now," Benny said.

"What is it?" Melanie asked, coming into the office. "What's going on?"

"I'm not sure," Thomes said. "But you were right. Something is going on, and I have a very bad feeling about it."

+++

Val made his way to the address he'd been given. It was a phone booth, as he suspected it would be. He found another cell phone taped to the underside of the shelf. It was wrapped in a piece of paper on which a phone number was written, so he dialed it.

"Hello," a voice said.

"Right," Val said. "I'm here. You're not very trusting, are you?"

"No."

"What about Susanne? Where is she?" Val asked.

"She's safe. And as soon as you give yourself up to us, she goes free."

"Forgive me if I don't take your word for that," Val said.

"You don't trust me. I'm hurt," the man said.

"Not half as much as you're going to hurt if you're lying to me," Val replied.

"Wait a moment," the man said.

There was a pause, and then Val heard Susanne's voice. "Just what the hell is going on? Who are these people? I was leaving my apartment on my way to work when I was grabbed from behind. A bag was pulled over my head, and I was brought here. Wherever here is."

"Never mind that now. Are you, all right?"

"Yes, I'm fine But—"

"Where are you?" Val cut in.

"I don't know. As I said, they put a bag over my head so I couldn't see."

While Val was talking to Susanne, a car pulled up and two men with guns got out. "Okay, hard-ass, get in the car," one of the men said.

Val looked at the men and then at their guns. He still had the phone in his ear.

"What's going on?" Susanne asked.

"Get in the car!" the man said again, gesturing with his gun

"I'll talk to you soon," Val said, and he hung up.

"I won't tell you again," the man said.

Val looked the man up and down. "You need to learn some manners."

The man hit Val with his gun. "You want to get the lead out!"

Val looked at the man but said nothing. He got into the car. The men got in with him, and they drove him to a house near Spring Valley Park. He was led into a room where his old adversary Luciano was sitting. Val had seen photos of him, but this was their first meeting in person. Even seated he looked to be about six foot three or four. He had long brown hair tied back with rawhide. His eyes were the darkest brown Val had ever seen.

"Ah, here you are! It's good to meet you, at last, Mr. Frankland. Or do you mind if I call you Val?"

"You can call me whatever you like. Just don't call me late for breakfast," Val replied.

Luciano waved his arm around the room. "I would like to welcome you to my humble abode."

Val looked around. "I would have a word with your decorator. Or even better, hire a new one."

"Ah, yes, the famous Val Frankland wit," Luciano said

"That's great. Now, where's Susanne?" Val demanded.

"She's safe, just as I said," Luciano replied.

"I would like to see her, to say goodbye."

"Yes, of course. I'm a man of my word. One of my associates will take you to her so you can say your goodbyes."

"Then you'll let her go as you promised?"

"Of course. Just as I promised."

One of the men who had brought him to this house leveled his gun at Val. "Come with me," he said.

Val walked in front of the man, who guided him up a flight of stairs to a doorway. The man pushed Val into the room. Susanne was tied to a chair. Her head was covered with a cloth bag.

"Who's there?" she asked. She sounded scared.

Val knelt in front of her and lifted the front of the bag. She kept her eyes tightly shut. "It's me," Val said.

Susanne opened her eyes a little just in case her captors were playing games with her.

"Yes, it is me." He leaned forward and kissed her.

"Come on! Untie me! Let's get out of here!"

Val shook his head. "No. I'm sorry I can't do that. If we tried that, they would kill us both. Luciano has agreed to let you go."

"No! Not without you!" Susanne said.

Val leaned forward again. She felt him put something into her pocket. He pulled away and smiled at her. "I'm going to pull this bag back down now. They'll be coming for me soon."

"Please, Val. We can both get out of here."

"Please just do as I ask. Trust me."

There was a knock on the door, and Val adjusted the bag over Susanne's head.

Val was taken back downstairs and into the room where Luciano was waiting.

"Are you happy now you've seen your lovely lady?"

"Yes, and I'll be happier when you let her go. Like you promised."

"Yes, yes. Just to prove to you that I'm not the bad man you think I am." He nodded to another of his men, who left the room. "Now what shall we talk about while we wait?" Luciano said.

"We could talk about who sold me out," Val said.

"What makes you think someone sold you out?" Luciano asked, smiling.

"Oh, come on. Please! There were very few people who knew that I wasn't dead, so which one of them do I have to thank?"

"It seems that you have a lot of enemies, Val. Some of them within your team."

"That maybe so, but it doesn't answer the question. Who was it?"

+++

Three hours later, Val was still sitting with Luciano. The situation was becoming tense. The phone in Val's pocket suddenly began to ring. Val looked at his watch. *It must be Susanne*, he thought.

Luciano and his men looked at Val. "Seems you have a call. Aren't you going to answer it? It might be important."

+++

Susanne had been taken to the outskirts of town. One of the men had cut the bindings on her hands and had then roughly pushed her out of the car onto the sidewalk in a small street where there were a few shops. She sat there for a moment as the car drove away. She lifted the bag from her head and looked around. She knew where she was, but she had no money, so she couldn't get back to the office. After she eventually managed to talk one of the nearby shopkeepers into letting her use the phone, she called the office and spoke to Thomes. She told him everything she could about what had happened. Thomes told her to stay where she was. He would send someone to get her. After what seemed like days, Benny turned up and took her back to the office. As soon as she walked in Thomes was there. "What happened?" he asked.

Susanne told him how some men had come to her apartment, how they had put a bag over her head, and how they had taken her with them.

"Do you have any idea where they took you?" Thomes asked.

Susanne shook her head. "No. Sorry. I had a bag over my head during the journey. Then I was kept tied to a chair, and they never removed the bag. Then Val came in. We talked. After he left, they put me in the car and dumped me where Benny picked me up."

"Do you remember any smells? Sounds? Anything?"

Susanne shook her head. "No. Sorry." She put her hand in her pocket and pulled out the paper Val had put there. She looked at the number and realized what it was. She turned to Benny. "Give me your phone," she said. Benny looked at her. She held out her hand, and Benny handed over his phone. Susanne punched in the number and pressed the call button. She heard the phone ring.

+++

Val took the phone from his pocket and pressed the answer button. As he had thought, it was Susanne.

"Please tell me what the hell is going! And, where are you?" Susanne almost shouted.

"Slow down. Are you all right?" Val asked.

"Yes, I'm fine. But—"

Then Susanne was gone and Thomes came on the phone. "Where the hell are you?" he asked.

"Dex!" Val exclaimed. "How are you?"

"Cut the shit," Thomes said. "Just tell me where you are and what the fuck is going on."

"You know I can't do that, but this is something I have to do," Val said. "You know that. I tried to do things your way—and look at what happened. People I love were put in danger. So now I'm going to do things my way. Please don't try to find me. It's much too late for that. This ends now. And before I go, I just want to say that you were right—some things and some people never change. Now, before I go, I have to ask for one last favor." There were tears in his voice. "Please tell Susanne that I do love her, and I sorry that it worked out like this. But there is no other way. Please ask her to forgive me." Then he hung up.

+++

"No! Don't you dare—" Thomes shouted. But it was too late. Val was gone.

"What was that about?" Susanne asked.

"He hung up on me," Thomes said. "The son of a bitch hung up on me."

"So, what's going on? Did he tell you?" Susanne asked.

Thomes nodded. "It would seem that he's made a deal with whomever it was that took you, if they let you go, he'd give himself up to them."

"We have to stop him! They'll kill him!"

"I wouldn't worry too much on that score. Remember whom we're talking about. You might be better off feeling sorry for the people who have him. He wouldn't have just given himself up without some kind of plan. He knows what he's doing." *I hope to god that he knows what he's doing,* Thomes thought, but he didn't say it out loud.

Thomes looked at the crumpled piece of paper in his hand. He unfolded it and found the note Val had written

I am sorry, boss. I thought I could change, but it seems that you were right a leopard can never change its spots. We are what we are. I made a big mistake by thinking that I could change, and it almost cost the person I love most in this world her life. Please tell her that I do love her, and I wish that things could have been different, but I don't have any choice. Now, this is going to finish, and I'm going to finish it my way. I will take care of things in the way I know best. Roger Ramjet's last crusade so to speak. Ha, ha. Please try to forgive me, and then perhaps it's best if you forget me.

Val

Thomes just stood there. He was shaking with anger.

"What is it?" Susanne asked.

Thomes didn't answer. She took the piece of paper from his hand and read it. "What does this mean? And what does he mean, we should try to forget him?" Susanne said.

"It means they intend to kill him," Benny said. "Now they have him, and they're going to kill him."

"They must have known where he was," Thomes said. "They knew somehow."

"No, that's impossible. No one could have known," Susanne said.

"Someone told them," Thomes said. "Someone sold him out."

"What will happen now?" she asked.

"You don't need me to tell you that," Thomes said.

"Then we have to find him," she said.

"Yes," Thomes said. "We do." As he turned away he said. "And God helps whomever it is who has him."

+++

"It's a shame that we never met in person before," Luciano said.

"Yeah, I tried to arrange meetings before," Val said. "Once in Paris and then again in New York."

"Yes, you did, but circumstances prevented us from meeting on both occasions."

"You mean that you ran away like the chicken shit coward you are," Val said.

One of the men who had brought him in stepped up behind Val and hit him on the back of the head.

Val turned and looked into the man's eyes. "That's twice," he said. "And for that, I'm going to kill you last. And I'm going to make sure that it's slow."

"That's enough of that," Luciano said. "I'm sorry about that. You will have to excuse my men. They need to learn some manners."

"Yeah, I know what you mean. Good help is so hard to find these days. You just can't find decent goons anywhere."

Luciano smiled. "But as I said, you have a lot of enemies—even, it seems, within your team. Now I would love to stay and chat some more, but I'm afraid I have other pressing engagements." He took a gun from his shoulder holster and pointed it at Val. "My men will take care of you. Or should I say they'll take care of your body? Now I must say that I have enjoyed our brief meeting and our little chat, but the time has come to say goodbye."

"Well maybe next time," Val said.

Luciano laughed. "I like your style and optimism, but I'm afraid that there will not be another time. This will be our first and only meeting. Goodbye, Val."

CHAPTER 13

Time to Die

What happened next happened fast. Val moved with a speed that left the mind behind. He spun around and grabbed the hand of the man who had hit him across the face. He put his hand over the man's gun hand, pointed the weapon at the man's partner, and pulled the trigger twice. The goon's chest exploded as he fell. Then Val broke the wrist of the goon he was holding and turned so he could look into the man's face. "I told you I would kill you last." He struck the man in the throat and left him to choke to death on his blood. "And I told you it would be slow."

Val picked up one of the guns and turned to where Luciano had been, but Luciano was gone. Luciano had seen Val's moves, but he hadn't been able to believe it. His men had told him how fast Val was, but he thought it was just their excuse for not being able to kill him. Val had moved too fast for him to get a shot off, so Luciano had decided that discretion was the better part of valor. After all, he who fights and runs away lives to fight another day. *Next time, Mr. Frankland, next time,* Luciano said to himself as he slinked away.

"Oh no, you don't!" Val shouted. "Not this time! This time it ends!"

More of Luciano's men appeared, and Val fought his way through them. He finally found himself in the park. He had to find Luciano. He had to end this, and if that meant giving his life to see it ended, then so be it. At least he would die with the knowledge that Luciano was dead and Susanne was safe.

+++

Thomes and the team had gone back to the office. Ricardo sat at his desk with the phone to his ear nodding his head and saying things like "Yeah", "Uh-huh", and "Okay".

"We need to find Val as quickly as possible," Thomes said. "Does anyone have any ideas? What about you, Ricardo. What was that call?"

"Sorry, boss. I was just making some calls to see if I could get any leads, but nothing." *There was nothing all right*, Ricardo thought. *I wouldn't waste my time looking for that shithead. Pretty soon he'll be dead anyway.* But didn't say any of this out loud.

"We need to find Val as quickly as possible," Thomes said. "Does anyone have any ideas?"

"Maybe I can trace the number of that phone you found—the one Val called from," Benny said.

"Then why are you still standing here talking about it?"

The director came down from her office to see what was going on. "So, do you think someone here gave him up?" she asked.

"It sure looks that way. Don't you think?" said Thomes.

"Do you have any ideas as to who it might be?"

"No not at the moment. But someone must-have. How else could they have found him?"

"I think I have something," Benny called.

"What have you got?" Thomes asked.

"It's not an exact location, but I think I can get close."

"Then get close," Thomes said.

Just then Agent Trent Ori came in looking for Thomes.

"What can I do for you, Trent?" Thomes asked. "I'm kind of busy just now."

"It might be what I can do for you," Trent said.

Thomes looked up at him. "And just what is it that you think you can do for me?"

"We just got a report of a massive disturbance at Rock Creek Park, and from the description, it sounds very much like Val Frankland. But since Val is dead, I thought I would ask if you know anyone who looks like him and can cause chaos and destruction like him."

"That is him!" Thomes said.

"It looks like he's come back from the dead then," said Agent Ori. "Either that or he's very lively for a corpse."

"Yeah, well you know what he's like. He never would just lie down," Thomes said.

"So it seems. Anyway, I've managed to keep the local cops out of it for now, but I don't know how much longer I can keep them out. If there's any gunfire, they'll move in, so you had better get Val out of there quickly."

"Thanks," Thomes said. "I owe you."

"You're welcome. And don't think I won't collect."

"Right," Thomes said to his team. "We know where Val is. Let's go!"

"How are you going to bring him in?" Trena asked. "If he's in full flow, so to speak, there's only one way to stop him, and that is to shoot him. And even that isn't easy."

"I have an idea about that," Thomes said. "Don't worry."

They all rushed out, Thomes in the lead. When Trena told Doc and Melanie what was happening they insisted on going along with them.

"We might as well all go. They might need some backup," Trena said.

When they got to the park, what they saw amazed everyone but Thomes. It was Val, all right, and he was taking no prisoners. Before they left the office, Thomes had called for police backup. He had told them to surround the park and to arrest anyone trying to leave. He told them not to move in unless he called them or they heard gunfire.

"Oh, my god," Susanne said. "When you said he was good, I never realized just how good. I mean, I know we saw him on the assault course, but this is for real, and I've never anyone so fast."

Melanie turned to Ricardo. "Now do you see why I told you not to try to take him on?"

Thomes turned to Susanne. "Are you afraid of Val?" he asked.

"No, of course not. Why would I be afraid of him?"

"What I have in mind sounds crazy, but it might work. Do you believe that he would ever hurt you?"

"No, of course not. Why?"

"If the police get into this, they will just shoot him to stop him. There is only one person in the world who can stop him now."

"Who's that, boss?" Benny asked. "Is it you?"

"No," Thomes said. "Even I couldn't stop him now—not without shooting him. No, the only person who can stop him now is Susanne."

"Me?" she said, sounding shocked. "How can I stop him?"

"Yes, you—if you're willing to try."

"Of course I am. Just tell me what I have to do."

"It's very easy. Just walk up to him and tell him to stop."

"Just tell him to stop?" Ricardo said. "That sounds like a good way for her to get killed. He's destroying anything that gets near him—in case you haven't noticed."

"Yes, I've noticed," Thomes said. "I know what he's doing, but I also know him." He looked at Susanne. "Trust me. If you walk up to him, calling his name as you get close, he will stop. Are you willing to give it a try?"

"Yes. Of course, I am," she said.

"Well then, the sooner the better. Remember, call his name as you approach him and tell him to stop."

"Okay." She turned and set off to where the action was.

Thomes turned to Benny and Ricardo. "Keep an eye on her. But don't shoot unless you have no other choice. Understood?"

"Understood." They set off to follow her. They split up so they could flank her.

Thomes watched as Susanne approached Val. She was brave, he had to give her that. She walked straight up to him, and he heard her call his name: "Valentine Frankland, you stop this right now."

It was like watching a toy robot slow down as the batteries lost power. He just stopped slowly and stood there blinking.

+++

Val saw Susanne, but he couldn't believe what he was seeing. At first, he thought he might be dreaming. How could Susanne be here?

But there she was, standing right in front of him. "Susanne?" he said. "What are you doing here?"

"I came to bring you home. I told you if you didn't come back, that I would come and get you."

Then Val heard another voice. A familiar voice. "Susanne, look out!" Benny called.

Val reached out and gently pushed Susanne to one side. Ricardo stood there, pointing his gun at him. "So it was you all along," Val said. "I should have known."

"Yes, maybe you should have. It just goes to show you're not as smart as everyone thinks you are."

"What the hell do you think you're doing?" Susanne shouted.

"Something I should have done when he first showed up," said Ricardo. "I thought I could rely on other people to do the job, but if you want something done right, you have to do it yourself."

"Don't be a fool," Val said. "Put the gun down."

Ricardo shook his head. "I don't think so."

"If you pull that trigger, you will die as well," Val told him.

"That doesn't matter. If I can't have Susanne, what is there to live for?"

"No!" Susanne shouted. But she was too late.

"Val saw the puff of smoke from Ricardo's gun just before he felt something hit him in the chest like a hammer. Simultaneously, he heard the flat bang. He fell to his knees, and Ricardo fired again. This time Val saw nothing but a bright light—then there was nothing.

+++

Susanne couldn't believe what she was seeing. She stood there in a state of shock. She had just seen Ricardo shoot Val, and now he was turning his gun towards her. Still, she couldn't move. She saw Benny, his gun still pointing at Ricardo. Benny called for Ricardo to drop his weapon, but Ricardo did not take any notice. Susanne was still transfixed as Ricardo seemed to be preparing to shoot. Benny didn't hesitate. If he had, she would have been dead. He fired three times, and Ricardo fell. She felt like being sick. *This just cannot be happening*, she thought. But, unfortunately, it was all too real.

Susanne finally got her legs to move. She went to where Val lay. She dropped to her knees beside him. She didn't know what to do. Should she move him? She didn't want to lift his head. That might cause further injury. *I can't hurt him any more than he's hurt already*, she thought.

+++

Benny could hear Susanne calling Val's name over and over. He ran to where Ricardo lay. Still pointing his gun, he kicked Ricardo's gun away and then put his fingers under the jaw of the man he had thought was his friend. Nothing. Ricardo was dead. Susanne knelt with Val's head resting on her knees. Benny could see the blood on Val's chest. His face was also covered in blood. One of Ricardo's bullets had hit him in the head. *Damn! I was too late*, he thought. *I was too goddamned slow.*

Police officers were arriving on the scene. Benny held up his badge. "Federal officer!" he shouted.

Thomes, Trena, Doc, and Melanie ran towards him. Melanie ran straight past him to where Susanne still knelt with Val's head on her knees. She looked down at Val and cried out. She knelt with Susanne. Both of them were crying. Melanie put her fingers to his neck. "He's still alive!" she shouted. "Hurry up with that ambulance!"

As Susanne and Melanie hovered over Val, Thomes, Trena, Doc, and Melanie stood looking on. "What happened?" Doc asked. "Just what the hell happened?"

"I don't know," Benny said. "I was just following Thomes's orders to keep Susanne covered. Then I saw Ricardo pointing his gun at Susanne and Val, so I shouted to Susanne to get down. Then I saw Val push her to one side. Then Val said, 'It was you'—or something like that—and Ricardo fired at him. I saw Val's body jerk, and he fell to his knees. Then Ricardo fired again, and Val's head jerked back, and he fell back. I shouted for Ricardo to drop his weapon, but he turned to fire at Susanne, so I shot him. I was too slow to save poor Val." Poor Benny looked as though he might cry, pass out, or both. "If I had seen Ricardo sooner and fired sooner I might have saved Val."

"No," Thomes said. "You did it right. You couldn't have done anything else. Don't you go blaming yourself."

The ambulance arrived to take Val to the hospital. Both Susanne and Melanie went with him. The others followed.

+++

Once again, the entire group was sitting in the hospital waiting room. No one spoke. Val was in surgery. "Déjà vu, anyone?" Doc finally said.

They all looked up at him but still, no one spoke. After what seemed like a lifetime the doctor came in and asked if there was a relative present. Susanne stood up. "I'm his wife," she said. How is he?" The others gathered around her.

"Well, I have some good news and some bad news," the doctor said. "The good news is that he is still alive. The bullet that hit him in the chest somehow missed anything vital and exited through his back. He was lucky with the bullet that hit him in the head—if you can call getting shot in the head lucky. It hit the side of his skull, tearing a section of it away exposing part of his brain. We can, of course, repair his skull with metal plates. I think I can safely say he seems to have a charmed life. Now, although his injuries are severe, he has a very good chance of survival."

"What about the bad news?" she asked.

"Well, as it is with so many head wounds, it is very difficult to say what's going on in his brain. We'll have to wait until he wakes up before we know any more."

"So what are you saying?" Susanne asked. "That he will survive but he could be brain-damaged?" The doctor looked down at his feet. "Please just tell me," she said.

"Unfortunately, we have no way of knowing for sure until he wakes up. He might be fine, but you must also prepare yourself for the worst. He could have brain damage, and he could well be left in a permanent vegetative state."

Susanne staggered, and Melanie grabbed her before she could fall.

"Thank you, doctor," Thomes said. "How long before we can see him?"

"Once we have him settled in his room, I will send a nurse to fetch you."

After what felt like hours, a nurse-leads them to the room where Val lay. As they entered the room, they saw him lying there with a lop-sided bandage around his head and another bandage around his chest. It hurt Susanne to see him like that, but she didn't hesitate. She went straight to his side and took his hand. The others followed her in and stood silently around them. The only sound was the rhythmic whoosh from the machine that was helping Val to breathe. Susanne sat beside him. She was crying. Melanie and Trena were both crying as they came to her side.

"He's strong," Trena said. "He's going to be okay. He loves you, and he'll fight his way back to you."

"He has to come back," Susanne said, still crying. "I need him. Just how am I supposed to raise the children without him?"

The two women looked at each other and then at Susanne.

"Children? What children?" Melanie asked.

"I'm pregnant," Susanne said.

"Pregnant? Does he know?" Trena asked.

"No. With everything that has been going on, I didn't get the chance to tell him."

"Then God will have to bring him back to you. He just has to," Trena said.

"Not a child. Children. I'm having twins."

"Are you sure?" Melanie asked.

Susanne nodded. "That's what the doctor told me."

"I don't know how to feel," Melanie said. "Sad about Val, but happy about the babies."

"Trena's right," Thomes said. "Val is strong, and he loves you. He knows that you love him. He'll fight his way back to you.

Susanne told the others that she would stay with him. With great sadness, the rest of them left her alone with Val.

CHAPTER 14

The Rocky Road Back

Val lapsed into a coma and stayed there for the next six months. Susanne stayed with him for most of that time. She talked to him and read to him. She told him what the weather was doing. She held his hand and even played music for him.

When Thomes came in with the doctor one day, she knew something was going on. "What is it? What's wrong?"

"Nothing is wrong," Thomes said. "But the doctors feel that maybe it's time to turn off his life support."

"No! Not!" she said. "That will kill him!"

"Listen, Susanne, I know Val better than most, and I know that he wouldn't want to go on like this with a machine doing his breathing for him. We have to let him go. This isn't living. This is just existing. A machine is breathing for him while his body wastes away. It keeps his heart beating for nothing."

"Nothing? What do you mean for nothing?"

"Look, I know you think I don't care, but we were like brothers—we *were* brothers—and I do care. I can't just stand by and watch him waste away like this. We have to let him go with dignity."

Susanne was crying again. "What am I going to do?"

"We have to be strong," Thomes said. "This is what he would want."

"Can I stay with him?" she asked.

"Yes, of course, you can. Once they have removed his ventilator, you can stay with him until the end, if that's what you want."

"Yes, that's what I want."

They left the room while the nurses removed the machine that was helping Val to breathe. Once that was done, Susanne and Thomes went back into the room. The doctor came to speak to them. "We have left his feeding tube in, for now, just in case he manages to keep breathing on his own. We can remove that later if we need to."

"It's not fair," Susanne said. "He's suffered for most of his life. He was forced into becoming something that he didn't want to be and never really was."

"Remember what he wrote," Thomes said. "He said he couldn't change what he was."

"That is a load of bull, and you know it. You keep telling me how well you know him, but you don't seem to know him at all. I have only known him for a short length of time, and in that short time, I've seen both sides of him. The real Val—the one that he tries to keep hidden— is soft, loving, and caring. You must have seen that side of him. After all, he married your sister."

"Yes, I've seen that person, but that was a long time ago. That person died in the same explosion that killed my sister, his wife. He died, and the new Val was born. He became someone else. He turned into what he is now."

"But that is not the *real* Val," she said. "Haven't you been listening? For all the years you have known him, you don't *know* him at all," she said. "Not really. I know you care about him, but that isn't the same as knowing and understanding him."

With the ventilator removed, it was quiet in the room. Susanne and Val were alone. She was sitting beside him listening to him breathe. She rested her head on his chest, listening to the slow, steady beat of his heart and his slow ragged breathing. She talked to him. She told him how much she loved him. She told him how much she needed him to help her with the babies. She told him how much they would need their dad.

The others came and went, but Susanne stayed at his side. If he came back, she wanted to be there. If, on the other hand, he died, she didn't want him to go alone. He looked so pale and vulnerable lying there, and she was determined that she would not leave him. But if nothing happened soon, she would have to leave him. Either that or she would have the babies there at his bedside.

Late one evening, Susanne was in her normal position, sitting beside him with her head resting on his chest. She was listening to the slow rhythmic beating of his heart. His breathing had returned to a slow, steady rhythm. She was almost asleep when she heard a croak and felt his hand tighten ever so slightly on hers. She sat up and looked at him. He seemed to be trying to speak, but no words came out. She put her finger to his lips. "Shush. Relax," she whispered. She pressed the call button for the nurse.

"Yes? Can I get you anything?" asked the nurse.

"Val just woke up."

"I'll get the doctor," she said and quickly left again.

While she was gone, Susanne got an ice cube from the pitcher next to the bed and rubbed it on his lips. *Just like last time*, she thought. It sounded as if he was still trying to speak. "What are you trying to say?" she asked.

His eyes closed again. When the doctor came in, he looked at Val. "Did he say anything?" he asked.

"He didn't speak. He just kind of croaked and then he closed his eyes again."

The doctor picked up the syringe the nurse had brought.

"What's that?" Susanne asked.

"It's just a mild sedative to help him relax." He injected the contents into Val's IV. "He will probably be in and out for a while. Until he's fully awake, we won't know what damage the bullet caused, if any."

Susanne sat looking at Val. She didn't know what to feel. All this time she has been praying for him to wake up, and now that he had, she was scared. What if that bullet had caused the severe brain damage the doctor had talked about? What would she do? She thought maybe they should have removed the feeding tube when they removed the ventilator. She hated herself for thinking like that, but what kind of life would it be for him, just lying there not knowing who he was or why he was there?

She was resting her head on him crying softly when he woke up again. He tried to speak again, but it still came out as only a croak. She looked at him. "What are you trying to say?"

"Baby," he croaked.

"Baby? What do you mean?" She wondered if he somehow knew she was pregnant.

"I hope you're not being a crybaby," he managed.

The tears came faster now. "Yes, I am," she cried.

He tried to laugh.

"If you laugh I'm going to hit you," she said.

"What happened?" he croaked. "Did I have an accident?"

"Something like that. I thought I had lost you!"

"No chance. You can't get rid of me that easily," he managed.

"I love you so much." She could see he was struggling to talk. "Shush," she said. "Don't try to talk anymore. Just rest." He started to say something, but she put her finger to his lips. "Rest," she said. "There will be time to talk later."

When she removed her finger, he croaked, "I love you."

+++

The next morning, Thomes and Trena came to visit. "How is he?" Thomes asked.

"He woke up a little while ago, and he recognized me," Susanne said. "But he doesn't remember what happened to him."

"I think that's for the best, don't you? But how about you? How do you feel?" asked Thomes.

"I feel better now that he's awake and seems okay. No sign of brain damage."

"Melanie will be here soon," said Trena. "She will be over the moon. So how are the twins doing?"

Susanne put her hand to her belly. "Lively as ever. I think they must be boys. By the way, they're kicking, I'm guessing they're practicing for the soccer team."

+++

The next few weeks were tough for Val. He kept forgetting things. When he got out of bed for the first time, he got a good look at Susanne. He saw the bump in her belly. He looked at her, his eyebrows raised.

She nodded, put her hand on her belly, and smiled. "You're going to be a daddy," she said.

Val's face didn't change. He just looked at her. Susanne thought he was angry. Then he smiled, and his whole face lit up. "I'm going to be a daddy," he said. Val looked up at Thomes who had just come in with Trena. "I'm going to be a daddy," he said, still with a big goofy grin on his face.

Thomes and Trena both smiled back at him. "Yes, we know," said Thomes

"I think they'll keep you busy," said Trena.

"Yes, I'm sure they will," Val said, still smiling.

"So, apart from that, how are you doing?" Thomes asked.

"I think I'm getting there," Val said.

They all chatted for a while, and then Thomes and Trena left the happy love birds alone.

Val's muscles had wasted a little, and he had to start rebuilding them again. The effort and frustration were written all over his face, but he was determined to be back on his feet and walking without any aids when his children were born.

Susanne continued to sit at his bedside, or next to him when he was in his wheelchair, constantly bringing him up to date with what had happened while he was sleeping.

"Can I ask you something?" he said one afternoon.

"Of course you can. Anything."

"What did I do?"

Susanne looked puzzled. "I don't understand what you mean." But she thought she did.

"I mean before this. I must have done something. I mean I know who you are, and when the others come to visit, I know them. So why can't I remember what I did or who I was?"

Susanne just sat looking at him.

"What?" he said. "What is it? Why can't I remember? What kind of accident did I have? I look down at my chest and I see scars that look suspiciously like bullet wounds. There are more scars on my stomach. There's what looks like a large groove on the side of my head, and I get severe pains in my head. So please tell me what I was and what happened to me."

"I can't tell you," Susanne said.

"What do you mean you can't tell me?" he shouted. "I want some answers. What is so bad that you can't tell me?"

"Calm down," she said. "You need to rest."

"I don't want to rest!" he shouted. "I want answers. I want to know what is going on. Why won't you tell me?"

The nurse came in. "Please, Mr. Frankland, calm down. You will make yourself ill."

"Stop telling me to calm down. I don't want to calm down. I want some answers."

The nurse left and returned with the doctor. "Now, Mr. Frankland," the doctor said. "I'm just going to give you an injection."

"And what is that for?" Val asked.

"It's something to help you relax. It may help you to remember things."

"You can forget that!" Val said.

"Please," Susanne said. She was crying hard now. "Please, Val, just let the doctor do it."

Val couldn't stand to see Susanne cry. Even though he was angry and upset, he relaxed and let the doctor give him the injection.

"What was that?" Susanne asked after Val had gone to sleep.

"It was just a sedative. He will be out for a few hours. What happened?"

"He can't remember what he did before all this happened."

"Have you thought about telling him?" the doctor asked.

Susanne just looked at him.

"Sorry," said the doctor. "Well, I think, for what it's worth, that it might not be the best idea to tell him what he wants to know. He's blocked it out of his conscious mind. Maybe it's too painful for him to remember, and his mind has shut it out to protect him from the painful memories. I'm sorry, but in my opinion, you shouldn't tell him what he wants to know. To do so could cause major problems."

"What do you mean major problems?"

"I mean that, if he has blocked it out because it's too painful for him, and you make him remember before he is ready to accept it, you might cause his mind to break down."

"But if he is asking, doesn't that mean he's ready to accept things?"

"No," the doctor said. "His conscious mind is asking, but his unconscious mind isn't ready to accept things yet."

"So what do we do?" Susanne asked. "We can't keep giving him injections to keep him asleep."

"You could always make something up."

"You mean lie to him?"

"Well, that's one solution," the doctor said.

When Thomes came to visit, Susanne told him what had happened and what the doctor had said.

"Don't worry about it," Thomes said. "I'll talk to him and explain things."

"But the doctor said we can't tell him."

"Don't worry. I'll make sure he's all right."

When Val woke up again, Thomes was sitting there. "Well, hello, and how are you feeling?" he asked.

"Pretty groggy. What did they give me?"

"I don't know what they gave you, but the doctor said the groggy feeling will pass. I understand you gave Susanne a hard time earlier."

"Yeah, I suppose I did. I'm sorry about that, but what would you have done in my place?"

"I suppose I might have done the same thing. Look, Susanne didn't tell you what you want to know because she doesn't know."

"Doesn't know?" Val said. "How can that be?"

"That is because you were a special investigator for the government. A special cop, if you like. Anyway, I thought we had a bad apple in my bunch, so you were brought in to try to find who it was because you were very good at that sort of thing."

"So, did I find them?"

"Yes, you did. And that is what caused your accident."

"I don't understand. How can finding a bad apple cause this?"

"Well, when you arrived in our offices—to your new assignment—Susanne fell for you big time. And you fell for her just as hard."

"Don't tell me she was the bad apple."

"No!" Thomes laughed. "Good God, no. The bad apple was an agent called Ricardo Belin. He also loved Susanne, but she wasn't attracted to him in the slightest. So, he decided to get rid of the competition and shut down the investigation in one fell swoop. To make a long story short, he shot you twice—once in the chest and once in the head."

"What happened to him?" Val asked.

"He was shot dead by Benny. He had to do it to save Susanne and himself. So you see, Susanne could have told you who shot you, but not what you did."

"I feel like such an ass," Val said.

"I can see why you would, but don't be too hard on yourself. Anyone would probably have reacted in the same way given the same circumstances."

"Where is Susanne now?"

"She's having a coffee with Trena. Do you want me to call her?"

"Yes, please. It seems that I some apologizing to do."

When Susanne came back, her eyes were red and puffy from crying. Thomes went out and left them alone.

"I'm so sorry. Can you ever forgive me? If you decide to tell me to go to hell, I'll understand."

She just stood at his bedside looking at him. "Just tell me that you love me," she said.

"You know that I love you."

"Yes, but I want to hear you say it."

"I love you very much. And I am so sorry for what I was earlier. I didn't know that you didn't know about me—about what I was."

"I still don't know anything about you."

"Well that makes two of us," Val said.

"What did Thomes tell you?"

"He said that I was some sort of special investigator brought in to find a dirty agent in his team and that the agent in question was called Ricardo and that he was in love with you, but you were in love with me."

"I could have told you that bit. About loving you, I mean."

He smiled at her. "Well, it seems this Ricardo set me up and then shot me. And then Benny shot and killed him. So, what do you think?"

"What do I think about what?" she asked teasing him.

"Do you think you can forgive me?"

"Oh, I don't know. I think I might be able to if you promise to love me forever."

Val smiled at her. "I hope that every promise I make is so easy to make and keep. My darling, I will love you forever and a day."

+++

When Susanne went into labor several days later, she was taken right from Val's room to the maternity unit. Val arrived shortly thereafter in his wheelchair.

"You don't have to be here if you don't want to," she said.

"But I do want to be here. And I have a surprise for you well."

"And what surprise is that?"

He stood up from his wheelchair and walked to her bedside.

"Is the rest of our lives going to be like this?" she asked.

"Like what, you pregnant and me running about in a wheelchair? No, I don't think so. It would be all right for a while, but then we would get too old or it would become boring."

"What am I going to do with you?" she asked.

"Oh, I'm sure I can think of something. Maybe even several somethings."

Val watched the birth of his children—a girl and a boy. As he held them, Susanne saw the tears in his eyes.

"I hope you're not going to be a crybaby when we're married," she said.

"I'll try my best not to be, but I can't promise. You did well. Just look at them—they're beautiful!" he said.

"I think I had a bit of help," she said, smiling.

"Yeah, but you did all the hard work. What are we going to call them?" he asked.

"Well, I thought that our little man should be called Valentine Dexter Donald Lewis." She looked at Val and began to laugh.

"What?" he said.

"Your face. It was a picture."

"Well, the poor little guy. He's so small. Do you think we should give him all those names to carry around?"

"I think he's going to be like his dad, so he will be strong enough."

"Okay, if you say so. What about our little princess?"

"If you don't mind, I think we should call her Melanie Trena Lilly."

"You forgot one name," he said.

"Oh yes. And what name is that?"

"Well, seeing that she is just as beautiful as her mother if you add Susanne, you've got a deal."

"Okay. We shall do as you wish, oh masterful one."

"And Thomes keeps telling me that I'm the nutty one!"

"You fool," she said.

He stuck his tongue out at her and blew a raspberry. Then a nurse came in. "There you are, Mr. Frankland. I've been looking for you. You have an appointment with your physical therapist!

"Oh no! Back to the torture chamber." Val walked across the room, dragging his leg making a noise like dragging chains across the floor. The nurse rolled her eyes at him, and Susanne laughed.

"What about your wheelchair?" the nurse asked.

"Are you going to push me?" Val asked.

"You've got no chance," the nurse said, laughing.

"You see what I have to put up with?" he said, and he mimicked the nurse rolling his eyes.

"Go on. Off you go to take your punishment," Susanne said.

Val kissed her and the babies. "See you later." Val went out pushing his wheelchair.

+++

Once Val had finished his session with the physical therapist, he went back to spend time with Susanne and his children. When Susanne finally fell asleep, he went to the nursery and just stood watching the babies sleep. He spent the time thinking about how he had never imagined that a life like this could be for him. During the night, when the twins woke up hungry and Susanne came to feed them, Val grabbed a bottle of formula and helped her. Once the babies were full and happy, Susanne kissed Val and said, "You should get some sleep."

Yeah, I will. I just want to stay here a little longer," he said, smiling.

Susanne went back to bed. When she woke in the morning, Val was still standing there beside the twins. "Have you been standing here all night?" she asked him. He nodded at her. She thought she

158

could see tears in his eyes. "Are you all right?" she asked him, sounding concerned.

He smiled at her. "Yes, I'm fine. I just can't believe that I'm standing here looking at my children."

She put her arm around his waist and rested her head against his shoulder. "Well, you are, and we will have a lifetime to watch them grow. Now you need to sleep."

"Yes, you're right," he said. He kissed Susanne and the babies and then went back to his room to get some sleep.

When he awoke, it was once again time for his session with his physical therapist. This was Val's hospital routine for the next four days. He had just finished his two-hour session with the physical therapist on the fourth day. The therapist was getting ready to leave when Trena, Thomes, and Benny walked.

"Hi," said Val. "If you're looking for Susanne, she's still in maternity."

"Yes, we know," Trena said. "We called in to see her on our way here. You have two beautiful children!"

"Thank you. So, if you don't want Susanne, it must be me you want."

"Sorry, Val, but yes," Trena said. "I'm afraid it is you we want. I'm here in my official capacity as head of the agency. Thomes is here as leader of the team you were attached to."

"So, what can I do for you, Madam Director and Special Agent Thomes?"

"I'm sorry that we have to do this. Valentine Frankland, you are under arrest under suspicion of your involvement in the deaths of several persons, one of them a federal agent. You do not have to say anything but anything you say can be used against you in a court of law. You have the right to an attorney if you cannot afford one, one will be appointed for you by the state. Do you understand these rights as I have read them to you?"

"This is a joke, right? You're kidding."

"Sorry, but this is no joke," said the director. "Agent Thomes, would you please take Mr. Frankland into custody."

"Okay," said Thomes. He turned to Val. "Agent Ferral here will escort you. Are you going to be a problem?"

Val just shook his head.

Melanie arrived just as they were putting the handcuffs on Val. "What are you doing? Why are you putting those on him?"

"I'm sorry, but Mr. Frankland is under arrest," Thomes said.

"Mr. Frankland? Under arrest? What the hell is going on? What are talking about?"

"I am sorry," Thomes said. "But this is how it is."

Benny looked very uncomfortable as he led Val out of the hospital to the car. "I'm sorry about this."

Val smiled. "Don't get yourself all upset. I know you have to do this."

Benny opened the car door. "Thanks," Val said as he handed Benny his handcuffs.

"Oh, thanks," Benny said. Then he stopped. "How did you do that?" he asked.

"Do you want to put them back on me?"

"There's no point is there? You would just take them off again, wouldn't you?"

Val just smiled but said nothing.

"Susanne is going to kill me for this," Benny said.

Val laughed. "She just might do that. But you won't be alone."

"By the way, I forgot to say congratulations. Have you thought of names for the babies yet?"

"Yes, we're going to call them Dexter and Lilly."

"You must both be so happy."

"Yes, we are."

"Susanne isn't going to be very happy about this."

"No, I don't suppose for one minute she will be. I don't think she will be happy at all."

CHAPTER 15

Happy Daze

To say that Susanne was not happy about Val's arrest was a bit like saying that Mount Everest was a bit of a hill. She stormed into Thomes' office like Hurricane Katrina. "Just what the hell is going on here?" she screamed at Thomes.

"Just calm down."

"Calm down?" she shouted. "Calm down? You arrested the man you said was your brother, the person who was responsible for the arrest of one of the most wanted men in the world along with most of his network of contacts. The fact that he almost died in the process doesn't seem to matter. Then you say 'Don't worry, Susanne, I'll make sure he's all right.' So, is this your definition of 'all right'?"

Thomes stood up. "Be quiet," he said. "No matter what he did or did not do, we still have to uphold the law. A lot of people died that day, and most of them were killed by Val. Also, he was witness to the shooting of a federal agent."

"I don't believe you," she said. "But I think I'm beginning to understand. He killed those men in self-defense, and you know it. Now please explain to me how he can be a witness to the shooting of Ricardo. Val had already been shot by Ricardo and was unconscious when Benny shot him. Even I didn't see exactly what happened because I was looking at Val. Remember when Val first got here? You were pissed off, and you tried everything you could think of to get rid of him, but that didn't work. So what happened then? Did you and the director get together and decide to use him as bait to get Luciano? After all, he had quit, so he was not part of your precious team anymore. If he got killed, it didn't matter. He was expendable. And if he survived, well, you could use this as an excuse to put him away so he couldn't come back and annoy you or get in your way anymore. Is that how it went?"

"No," Thomes said. "It wasn't like that at all. You are way off base, but it doesn't alter the fact that Val killed a lot of people, and he might have information about Ricardo. We know he was unconscious by the time Ricardo was shot, but he spoke to Ricardo, and he may have information that can help."

"But he can't remember. Don't you get it? He can't remember what happened. And do you remember what the doctor said? If you make him face things that he's forgotten before he's ready, you could destroy his mind."

"I'm sorry. But it's out of my hands. I still have to obey orders. Before you say anything else, Val would understand that this isn't personal, no matter what you might think."

"Then can I see him?"

"Of course you can. He's with the director at the moment. Shall we join them?"

They went back into the squad room where Susanne had left Benny looking after the twins. Thomes picked up Lilly and Susanne got Dexter.

"Are you sure you want to call him Dexter?" Thomes asked.

"Yes, of course, we are. Why? What's wrong with that?"

He sighed. "Nothing," he said. "Nothing. Come on, Princess, let's go and find your dad."

They made their way to the director's office where they found Val sitting talking to Trena. When they entered, Val stood, kissed Susanne, and took Dexter from her. Then Trena stood and took the baby from Val. "Thank you, but I think you'll find that he wants his Auntie Trena, don't you?" she said kissing Baby Dexter on his nose.

"Would someone please tell me just what the hell is going on here?" shouted Susanne. "First I am told that you have arrested Val. Then when I get here and start shouting, Thomes tells me it's out of his hands, so we come up here and I find him sitting drinking tea and chatting as though nothing has happened. So, come on, somebody please tell me what's happening."

"We had to arrest Val, but it was just a formality really," Trena said.

Thomes put his hand on Val's shoulder. "Come on," he said. "Lilly and I want to buy you a coffee."

Val looked at him with a puzzled expression on his face.

"I think we should leave the women to talk while we have coffee," suggested Thomes.

Val shrugged. "Okay. If you insist." He stood and gave Susanne and baby Dexter a kiss then left with Thomes and Lilly. Once they had left the room, Susanne turned to Trena.

"I don't understand," Susanne said.

"We now know that Ricardo was determined to kill Val. Just as we know that some of the deaths that day were caused by Luciano. Just as we know that Ricardo would have killed you if it hadn't been for Benny. From what we can figure out, it seems that Ricardo had decided he could never have the relationship with you that he wanted, and if he couldn't have you, then nobody else could either. We know that Benny was forced to shoot and kill Ricardo. It was justified, but we still had to arrest Val, bring him in, and ask him some questions."

"So, have you done that now?" Susanne asked.

"Yes, I have. And I'm satisfied that Ricardo and Luciano—or his men—were responsible for the deaths that day."

"You know, I hope that the rest of my life with Val isn't going to be like this."

Trena smiled. "With Val, you never know. It is so nice to them back together again. Dexter and Val—just like old times." Then she changed the subject. "When you came in, I was just offering Val a job."

"A job on the team?" Susanne asked.

"No, not on the team. I don't think he would want that. I was thinking more about a position in the training department. I would like Val to take charge of the training. There is no one better."

"Has he accepted?"

"No, not yet. He said he wanted to talk to you first. Something about being a kept man. Does that mean something to you?"

"Yes, it's one of the few things that does make sense."

"We'll just have to finish up the paperwork, and then Val will be cleared to take the position of head of training."

"Won't the fact that he can't remember what he did before affect his ability to train other people?" asked Susanne.

"I don't think so," said the director. "You see, Val is the best, and he would make a great teacher. But we will see. Now, I'm willing to release him into your care if you're willing to take responsibility for him."

"Yes, of course. I think I can do that." She looked around at the others, who had come into the room. "I think we might be having regular visitors," she said.

"I think you might have quite a houseful," Trena said, bouncing Dexter in her arms. And I haven't seen Doc so excited in years. Lewis and Lilly called Thomes to say they would be coming to visit their grandchildren."

Susanne laughed. "We are going to be busy, aren't we?"

It was Trena's turn to laugh. "Yes, I think you are. Now, I know Thomes has already said this, but thank you, Susanne, for saving Val."

"Like I told Thomes, I didn't do anything."

"But you did. You came into his life, and you were strong enough to hold him in yours. You never gave up on him."

"Why would I give up on him? I love him."

Trena smiled. "Yes, I know you do. When he first arrived, I had my doubts about him. Then he met you, and the change in him was amazing: he changed back to what he used to be before the bad times."

"Did you ever find out who attacked him?"

"Yes. The first attack was a couple of local thugs that Ricardo hired to take care of Val, but they failed, so Ricardo found one of the orderlies with a drug problem and paid him to try to poison him. When Val went to stay with Lewis and Lilly, Ricardo knew what was happening, so he contacted Luciano. He made a deal with him: Luciano got to kill Val, and Ricardo got you. That was the price for him giving up Val. You were to be the bait to lure Val into a trap. You would then be set free, and Val would be killed. But Ricardo didn't count on just how good Val is."

"Oh, God, that's sick. But I wouldn't have gone with Ricardo anyway. I mean I liked him, yes, but not like that."

"You know that, but in his mind, he believed that, if he removed Val from the picture, you would fall for him. You would see him as the white knight who rode in on the mighty charger to save the damsel fair. But it's all over now. You are with Val, and both of you are happy. I must say that, if anyone deserves happiness, it's Val."

"What was Val like when he was young?"

"Doc told you most of it at the hospital. But he was a lot like he is now. When Doc found him in his barn, Val was pretty messed up. But with time and Doc's help, love, and guidance, he turned into an amazing young man. He was good looking, intelligent, amusing ... I could go on, but I think you know all that."

"Yes, I do," Susanne said.

"Well, when he met Juliet he was lost. They pretended not to like each other. But the only people they were fooling were themselves."

"So, they didn't like each other at first?"

"Oh, yes, they did. They just pretended they didn't, but we all knew they did. They didn't fool anyone. Then one evening Val took Juliet out to dinner. He had been acting sort of nervous and on edge for most of that day. We asked him what was wrong, but he just brushed it aside saying it was nothing. Val picked Juliet up and took her to the restaurant. They had just ordered their meals when a guy appeared with a big bunch of flowers for Juliet. Val had ordered them to be delivered at the restaurant. Then Val got down on one knee and asked her to marry him. She told us later that she knew he was up to something, but she didn't expect that. She said she had tears in her eyes as she accepted. She couldn't help it. Then, to cap it all off, Val got up on stage and sang a song that he'd written for her called "Juliet." She was blown away. She said it was fantastic. The whole restaurant stood and applauded. The wedding itself was fantastic as well. Lewis and Lilly did them proud."

"But, sadly, as we know, the marriage didn't last very long, and that was what changed Val. The Val we had known and loved disappeared, and this new version of him appeared. The only way I can think of to describe the way changed is that it was like watching a butterfly emerge from its cocoon, only this butterfly was a mutant something like a cross between a butterfly and a killer hornet—beautiful but deadly.

"Do you have any photos of Juliet?" Susanne asked.

"I can do better than that," Trena said.

"How do you mean?"

"I mean that I have a video. They're both in it."

"Really?" Susanne said. "I would love to see that."

"Well, why don't we have dinner at my place? We can watch the video after we eat."

"That would be great. But what about Val? Do you think it will be okay for him to see it?"

"I think so. I don't think there's anything in it to upset him. But we can ask Doc for his advice before I suggest watching it. Come on." Trena said. "We had better go down to the squad room see what those two are up to."

+++

Trena and Susanne entered the squad room only to find that Val and Thomes weren't there. But they were in time to find Doc and Melanie standing over Benny demanding to know why Val had been arrested.

"Leave the poor man alone," Trena said. "You'll give him a complex."

Benny looked at Trena. She could see the relief in his face. "Val hasn't been arrested," she said.

"Where is he?" Doc asked.

Trena shrugged. "I don't know. Thomes took Lilly and Val to get coffee. I thought they meant here, but—"

"We've all been invited to Trena's for dinner tomorrow evening, " Susanne said. After we eat, she has a video to show us. Val doesn't know about it yet."

"It's an old video I have with all of us on it," Trena said. "But it has Val goofing around with Juliet. What do you think, Doc? Do you think it will be all right for him to watch that?"

Doc thought for a moment. "I think it should be safe enough, but we'll just have to keep an eye on him."

When Val, Thomes, and baby Dexter came back, Val kissed Susanne and Lilly.

"Where have you been?" Susanne asked him.

Val jerked his thumb towards Thomes. "Thomes took me to a coffee shop down the block. Nice coffee!"

The director has invited us to dinner at her house tomorrow evening. What do you think?"

"Sounds good to me. I'll look forward to it," Val said. "Is that just us or—"

"No, all of us," Susanne said.

"Oh, yay! A party!" Val said.

"Come on then," Susanne said. "I think we had better get the twins and go home or there will be no work done around here."

"Home," Val said.

"Yes, home. Are you all right?" Susanne asked him.

"Yes, it's just … oh, I don't know. I suppose I never think of anywhere as home anymore. Do you mean your place?"

"Yes, of course, I do. And it's our place now," Susanne said.

"Home," Val said again.

"Right. I am releasing Val into your care, so he is free to go."

"Thank you," Val said.

"You're here!" Melanie said.

Val patted himself. "Yes, I sure am."

"I mean you're not locked up or anything?"

"No, I'm not locked up or anything. Everything is okay now, but if I'm lucky, Susanne is going to take me home and discipline me."

Susanne looked him up and down. "You wish."

"Well, it was worth a try."

CHAPTER 16

The Headaches

"Come on, let's go home," Susanne said.

Home, Val thought. *Home. Why does that give me a funny feeling down my spine?*

"Is everything all right?" she asked him.

"Yes, I'm fine. I think things just started to gang up on me all at once. But I'm fine—honest."

"Are you sure?"

He smiled at her. "Yes, I'm sure." He put his lips close to her ear. "And later, when the kids are in bed, I would be happy to show you just how fine I feel."

As it turned out, she thought he must have felt fine indeed. When she awoke the next morning, she reached out for Val, but he wasn't there. "Val?" she called. There was no answer. She sat up, grabbed her robe, and left the bedroom. She found Val in the kitchen with the kids. He had made coffee and was starting breakfast. "You're up early," she said.

"Yeah. I heard Dexter. They were both awake, and I thought I would get up with them before they woke you. *We* thought you might like some extra sleep, isn't that right, kids?" The twins gurgled. "See? They agree with me."

She went over to him and kissed him and then the twins.

"Please, madam, no taking advantage of the staff while they are working."

What time do you get off?" she asked.

"Give me five minutes," he said.

"Fool," she said, laughing.

"Have you heard this?" he said to the twins. "Your mother is calling your dad a fool." The twins gurgled again. "You see? They agree with me again," he said, and he stuck his tongue out at her.

"You haven't forgotten about tonight, have you?" she asked.

"No, of course, I haven't."

She thought she saw that shadow cross his face again.

"Are you sure you still want to go?" she asked him.

"Yes, of course, I do. I'm looking forward to it."

She looked into his face. "If you're sure."

He kissed her. "Yes, I'm sure."

"Good. I'm looking forward to it."

"Me too."

At the end of the day, when it came time to get ready, Val said, "Do you think it might be better if I stay here with the kids and you go without me?"

"Why? Don't you feel well? I'll stay here with you if you want."

"It's nothing like that. I was just thinking that it might be a bit much for the twins, that's all."

"The twins will be fine," she said. "And don't start using them as an excuse. If they get tired, we will just let them conk out and go to sleep. You know as well as I do that, if I turn up without you and the twins, there is going to be a riot. But if you don't feel up to going, I'm sure they will all understand."

"No, it's nothing like that."

"Look, if you don't feel well, we can cancel and stay home." She felt his forehead.

"No, it's nothing. I'll be fine. Honest."

"Well, if you're sure."

Val kissed her. "Yes, I'm sure."

On the way to Trena's house, Val and Susanne picked up Benny from his home. Susanne and Benny had never been to Trena's house before. Trena lived in a large house in Georgetown on Foxhall Crescent. Susanne was enchanted by the house. To her, it looked like a castle from a fairy story—the one where the princess lives after she marries her prince charming. The thought made her smile.

"What?" Val asked her.

"Oh, nothing. I was just admiring the house, wondering what it would be like to live in a castle."

Val laughed. "I guess I'll just have to build you a castle, won't I?"

"Fool," Susanne said. "I didn't mean—"

Val cut her off with a kiss. "Wait until you see the inside."

The house had belonged to Trena's grandparents. It had been built to her grandad's specifications. When Trena's grandparents died, her mother and father hadn't wanted to live in the house. They said it was too old and too cold, so they had moved to California for the sunshine. Trena had two older brothers who hadn't wanted the house either, so Trena had inherited it and had lived there quite happily. By the time Val, Susanne, and Benny got to Trena's home, Doc and Melanie were already there. As soon as they stepped inside, Melanie grabbed the twins. "Come to Aunty Melanie. I'll take care of you," she said with a great big smile on her face.

Susanne and Benny looked around. The house was huge. The living room alone was bigger than Susanne's apartment. Benny whistled softly. Together Susanne and Benny looked at the photographs hanging on the walls. There was a picture of Trena with her family—her grandparents, parents, and her two brothers, Nicholas and Stuart. Susanne stopped in front of one of the photos and starred at it. Doc was standing behind her.

"Do you recognize anyone?" he asked, smiling.

"Is that the director?" she asked.

"Yes. Is that the only person you recognize?"

Susanne looked closer. "Val and Thomes?"

Doc nodded and waited for the next question. The photo Susanne was looking at was from a long time ago—Trena, Thomes with his girlfriend of the time, and Val standing with his arm around a young girl who could have been a young Susanne. Val was smiling.

"Who is that girl that Val has his arm around?" Susanne asked, even though she knew the answer to her question.

Doc thought maybe she sounded a little jealous. "That, my dear, is Juliet Thomes."

Susanne stared at the photo a while longer. Benny and Melanie came up behind her.

"Wow, you do look like sisters," Melanie said. Val came up behind her, put his arms around her waist, and kissed her neck. He looked at the picture. Doc was watching him, but he thought that Val was looking but not seeing.

Just then Trena announced that dinner was ready. They made their way into the dining room, which again was huge. Susanne noticed that there were more photos and paintings on the walls.

As they sat around the dinner table, Val began to laugh. He was watching Melanie try to eat while she had a baby on each knee. "I think we're going to have to feed you, never mind the twins," he said. "Here, let me take Lilly-bee, at least until you've finished eating."

"Lilly-bee?" Susanne said. "Where did that come from?"

Val looked dazed for a moment. Susanne stood, afraid that he was going to drop Lilly. "Val? Are you all right?"

Val shook his head as if to clear it. Then he pulled Lilly to him. "Sorry. I'm okay."

Everyone was looking at him with concern.

"I'm okay," he said again. "Honest."

Susanne sat back down. "If you're sure?"

"Yes, of course, I'm sure. Now, what were you saying?"

Susanne paused for a moment. "I asked where the name Lilly-bee came from."

"I just looked at her in that little black-and-yellow-striped dress and thought, *She looks just like a beautiful little bee.*"

Everyone laughed. There was general chatter as they ate. All the while, Susanne kept an eye on Val. Once the meal was over, everyone pitched in with the dishes. With that done and the after-dinner drinks made, they settled down to watch the video. Susanne sat at one end of the sofa. Val sat on the floor next to her with his head resting on her knees. Melanie sat with the twins on her lap. Trena started the video. A group of teenagers appeared on the screen, they were all fooling around and laughing. The boys were throwing a football around and the girls were laughing and cheering. Just before the moment when Val put his arms around Juliet and kissed her, Val stood up.

"Where are you going?" Susanne asked.

"Just to get a drink of water, that's all."

"Do you want me to pause it until you get back?" Trena asked.

"No, you don't have to. You carry on." He went into the kitchen.

Susanne stood to follow him, but Doc put his hand on her arm. "You keep watching. I'll make sure he's okay," he said.

"Are you sure?" Susanne asked.

"Yes, of course. It's all right. I've seen this before. I know how it ends." Doc went into the kitchen and saw Val standing by the back door with a glass in his hand. "That won't help," Doc said.

Val raised his glass. "Cheers. Lemonade," he said.

"I'm sorry," Doc said. "I thought … well, you know what I thought."

"Yes, and you don't have to apologize."

"What happened in there?"

"Nothing. It was nothing."

"And now? Is it the video?"

"I don't know," Val said. "I just felt … I'm not sure how to explain what I feel." He was rubbing his forehead.

"Are you sure you're all right?" Doc asked him.

"Yes. I guess it's just a bit of a headache."

"Have you been getting a lot of those?" Doc asked.

"A few. But the painkillers take care of it."

"You're looking tired as well. Has there been a lot of that too?"

"You know how it is. We seem to be up at all times with the twins. It's just broken sleep."

Doc searched in his bag, which he'd left by the door, and found him some tablets. "Here take these."

"Thanks," Val said, and he swallowed them with his drink.

Susanne came into the kitchen. "What are you two up to?" she asked.

"Not a lot," Doc said.

She looked at Val. "Are you sure you're all right?"

"Yeah. It's just a bit of a headache, but Doc found me a couple of painkillers. I'll be as right as rain in no time. Is the video over?"

"No, not yet. But I thought I should see what the two of you were up to."

"Nothing much," said Val. "Just plotting to take over the world— that's all."

She stuck her tongue out and made a face at him. "You are all right, then, aren't you?" she asked.

"Yes. I said I am."

"Okay, if you're sure." She left Doc and Val alone in the kitchen and went back to watch the rest of the video.

"That was a lie you told her," Doc said.

"I don't know what you're talking about."

"Yes, you do. Those headaches are worse than you're letting on, and they are more frequent, aren't they? I didn't know for sure until just now—not until you just lied to Susanne."

"I have no idea what you're talking about," Val said.

"Oh, yes you do. You might be able to fool Susanne, but you can't fool me as easily. For one thing, I'm a doctor. For another thing, I've known you a lot longer than she has. I raised you like my son, so please don't insult me by telling *me* lies."

"Okay, so the headaches are worse that I said, and I have a lot more of them, but if I had told Susanne, she would have nagged me to go see a doctor, and she'd never let me out of her sight."

"Yes, I think you're right. I believe she's a very smart girl. Now, will you listen to me? I want you to go see a doctor. I know a very good one."

"Please don't," Val said.

"Look," Doc said, "I don't care what you think. I care about you, and Susanne cares about you—even if you don't care."

"Stop it. Stop right there. You know I care. You have been like a father to me since I was twelve years old, and I love Susanne and the twins more than anything in this world."

"Then please do as I ask. Do it for them as well as for me. Then I'll be able to sleep at night."

"Okay, you win. Give me his name and number. I'll make an appointment."

"What appointment?" Susanne asked from behind them. Neither of them had heard her come back in.

"Val has been getting some bad headaches, so I want him to see a doctor just to be on the safe side."

"Is that what's wrong with you this evening?" she asked.

"Yes," he said.

"Why didn't you say so?"

"Because I didn't want to worry you or spoil your evening."

"So, you're going to make this appointment tomorrow," she said. It wasn't a question.

"Yes, of course, I will. I promise."

"Okay. Then I suppose that will have to do."

"So, to change the subject," asked Val, "what did you think of the video?"

"I think it was excellent." She turned to Val. "You were really good. You should have been a professional singer and dancer, or maybe a footballer."

Val just laughed.

+++

True to his word, Val called the doctor's office the next day. He used Doc's name and was told they could fit him in in about four weeks. Val said that would be fine and hung up. When he told Susanne that it would be four weeks before he could see the doctor, she thought it was a long time to wait. "It's just a few headaches," he told her. "No big deal."

But, by the time the four weeks were up, it was a big deal. The headaches had increased in intensity and frequency. Val saw Dr. Cuthbert, who gave him a thorough examination. He ordered blood tests and an MRI scan. Dr. Cuthbert said it would take a few days to get all the results back, and he arranged an appointment for the following week.

+++

The next time Val sat in Dr. Cuthbert's office, the doctor looked at him and said, "I have the results of all your tests, Mr. Frankland, and I am sorry to say they are not good. But then I think you already know that, didn't you?"

"Yes, I guess I do."

Dr. Cuthbert began to explain his findings, but Val held up his hand to stop him. "Please, Doctor, just give me the bottom line. How long do I have?"

"I'm sorry, but that isn't easy to say. First, we must aspirate the fluid that has built up in your cranial cavity. Then we will be able to get a better picture of what is happening and how fast it's happening."

"So how soon do you need to do this?" Val asked.

"The sooner the better. The longer you leave it, the worse the headaches will become, and survival will become more of an issue."

"So, if you had to guess, how long would you give me?"

"Look, Mr. Frankland, until we drain that fluid so we can see what's going on, I couldn't even begin to guess."

"Okay," Val said. "But one more thing—no one can know about this. I mean, people will find out about the drilling into my head and the draining of the fluid, but no one can know anything else—not my wife, and not even Doc Sibbald. Okay?"

"Certainly, Mr. Frankland. I would never even dream of discussing your case with anyone else. Not without your consent. The law protects your privacy."

"Thank you. Now when do you want to drill these holes in my head?"

"I think it might be for the best if we do it tomorrow. I'll meet you at the hospital at, say, ten in the morning. You should bring someone with you because you won't be able to drive after the anesthesia, and you might be feeling a bit nauseous."

Val called Doc on his way home to tell him what was going to happen. At home, as soon as he walked through the door, Susanne was there waiting. "Okay, come on. Tell me. What is it?"

"Can I come in first?" he said.

"Sorry, but I've been just sitting here worrying and waiting."

"All right, come and sit with me, and I will explain it as best I can. They have found a build-up of fluid in my head, and that is what is causing the headaches. So, the doctor is going to drill some holes in my head to let all the fluid out. That will relieve the pressure, and the headaches will go away."

"That sounds gross," she said. "Are they sure it will be safe?"

"The doctor said it will be fine. But I need someone to come with me to hold the bucket just in case there are any brains in there and they leak out."

She looked at him, her eyes wide. "You're kidding, right?"

He laughed. "Yes, but only about there being any brains in there. But seriously, I do need someone to come with me just in case I don't feel well enough to drive after the anesthesia."

"When is it?" she asked.

"Tomorrow morning. If you don't think you can handle it, I can ask Doc or Melanie."

"I'll be fine," she said. "But what about Dexter and Lilly?"

"I think Auntie Melanie would be happy to help there. I'll give her a call and ask her."

As it turned out, Melanie was over the moon about having Dexter and Lilly for the day. "So where are you guys going? Somewhere nice?" Val told her what was going to happen. Melanie became instantly concerned. "Are you sure that it's safe?" she asked.

"Yes, I'm sure it's safe. The doctor said I might feel a bit sick and dizzy, but that's all. Susanne is coming with me, so I'll be fine. As soon as everything is over, one of us will call you."

"Okay, but you had better call me. And if you don't feel well enough, you can leave the babies with me overnight."

"Thanks," Val said. "We'll drop Dexter and Lilly off in the morning on the way to the hospital."

"See you then," Melanie said.

"You sure will," Val said. "Bye for now."

"What did she say?" Susanne asked him.

"She's worried for me, but she says she will look after the twins. And if we want to, we can leave them with her overnight."

"What do you think?"

"I think it might be interesting—just the two of us with no kids to worry about."

"I suppose it could be fun. If you're up to it?"

"Madam, you underestimate my resilience," Val said. "Where are the children now?"

"They're sleeping at the moment. Why?"

He grabbed her and pulled her to him. "I'll show you up to it," he said.

"Oh, yes, please," she said.

Afterward, they were lying together on the bed when they heard Lilly wake up. Susanne started to get up, but Val put his hand on her arm. "I'll go," he said, and he picked up his robe." He came back with both twins in his arms.

"I didn't hear Dexter," she said.

"No, but he was checking out his toes, so I thought I'd better bring him along."

Just then Lilly reached up grabbed Val's lip and pulled it. "Blug," she said.

"Blug," echoed Dexter.

"Yes, blug," Val said.

Susanne was rolling around on the bed laughing.

"You see, kids? Do you see? Your mother is laughing at me in my moment of pain."

Both Lilly and Dexter goggled at Val and then began to gurgle at him.

"Looks like I'm outnumbered," he said, and he started laughing himself.

The next morning, they dropped the twins off with Melanie. When they got to her house, she was quiet not her usual bubbly self. "Are you all right?" Val asked her.

"Yes, I'm just worried about today."

Val hugged her. "Don't you worry. Susanne is with me, and she will make sure nothing goes wrong. Okay?"

"Yes. But give me a call as soon as you can, okay?"

"We will," said Val. "Well, it will more than likely be Susanne who calls, but I promise she will."

They arrived at the hospital, and while Susanne waited in the waiting room, Dr. Cuthbert performed the minor operation. He drained the fluid and removed some bone fragments. When it was over, he pronounced the procedure a success. Val came out with a huge bandage on his head.

Dr. Cuthbert followed Val into the waiting room and spoke to Susanne. "I want you to make sure he gets plenty of rest. If he gets more headaches, they will pass quickly. I would like to see him again in about a week."

"Excuse me," Val said. "But it was my *head* you drilled, not my ears. I can still hear you."

"Sorry. But if you would please call my office and make an appointment for next week, I will have a look at how things are doing."

For most of that week, Val seemed to sleep a lot. He didn't eat much. He just drank lots of water. Towards the end of that week, Val seemed to come back to himself a bit. "You don't have to come with me this time," he said to Susanne, referring to his follow-up appointment. "They're only going to change the dressing and see if the brain implant worked. If you and the twins would like to pick me up afterward, we can have some lunch."

Are you sure?" Susanne asked.

"Yes. The walk and the fresh air will do me good. Clear the cobwebs away."

"If you're sure," she said again.

"Yes, I'm sure." He kissed her and the twins.

"Do you think I should invite Melanie to lunch as a way to say thank you for looking after these two little rascals?"

"Yeah, sounds good. You could ask the others as well if they're free."

"That sounds like a good idea. I'll call them."

"Right. I'm going. I must say I'll be glad to get this bandage off."

"I've just got used to seeing you like that, oh great swami."

He stuck out his tongue and blew a raspberry.

Val arrived at Dr. Cuthbert's office and took a seat in the waiting room. After a while, a nurse took him into an examination room and changed his dressing. Then she showed him into Dr. Cuthbert's office. Val sat while the doctor looked at his notes.

"The wounds are healing just fine, but I'm afraid that is the only good news I have for you. Taking into account—"

Val held up his hands. "Please, just the short version—in simple English."

"Okay then. The short version is. I am sorry to have to tell you this, but you have a brain tumor, and there is nothing I can do about it. I'm afraid it's inoperable."

"So how long do I have?" Val asked him.

"It's not that simple, Mr. Frankland. It could be one year or five years, or it could be six months. There is just no way to predict exactly. I would like to refer you to an oncologist I know—a very good one. You and your wife could both get help and support in dealing with this—"

"No, thank you," Val said.

"Please, Mr. Frankland. I urge you to reconsider."

"There is no need to reconsider. This is what I want."

The doctor sighed. "Very well, as you wish. But if you should change your mind, please contact me. Sooner rather than later."

"Thank you, doctor, but I don't think I'll be changing my mind. Now, unless there's anything else, I am going to meet my wife for lunch."

"No, there's nothing else. Goodbye, Mr. Frankland."

Val left the doctor's office and sat outside to wait for Susanne.

"So how did it go?" Susanne asked when she drove up with the twins.

"It went very well. The doctor is very pleased with the way the holes in my head are healing. He wants me to go back in two weeks to have the dressings removed completely, and that will be that. He said that, if I do have any problems, I can call him, but I think once the dressings come off, that will be it."

"Are you sure?"

"Yes, I'm sure. Now can we please go get some food? I'm starving."

"You must be feeling better. Come on, let's get to the restaurant and tell everyone the good news," Susanne said.

They laughed together.

CHAPTER 17

Family Matters

When Val and Susanne arrive at the restaurant, the others were sitting around the table chatting and laughing. They all asked how Val's appointment had gone. Val said it had gone very well. Then lunch was brought out, and they all sat chatting and eating.

Val excused himself and went to the restroom, and Doc followed him. When they were washing their hands, Doc looked over at Val. "Is something wrong?" Val asked him.

"Not that I know of. But I was hoping that you would tell me what the doctor said."

"I have told you," Val said.

"No, you've told us what you thought we should hear. Now I would like you to tell me what he said."

"Are you calling me a liar?"

"Why should I be? You were never very good at lying. Maybe because you didn't tell lies."

"I have already told you."

"What you told me is bull. You know it, and I know it. We have had this conversation before. You are still my son, and the look in your eyes says that you're not telling us everything."

"I still can't fool you, can I?"

"No, you can't. You never could. Now please tell me. How long he gave you?"

"He doesn't know. It's a tumor, and it's inoperable. He said I could have ten years or ten days."

"Didn't he refer you to an oncologist?" Doc asked, sounding shocked.

"Yes. He offered to refer me, but I said no."

"Why in God's name did you say no? Some drugs could help."

"No. And, please—do not say a word to anyone," Val said.

"You have to tell Susanne the truth."

"No," Val said again, shaking his head. "What good would it do? She would just spend the next however many years worrying. At least this way it will be quite a few years before she has to deal with this." *I hope*, he thought. "Then when something happens, it will be quick. She will have the chance to grieve and move on. If I tell her now, she'll be grieving for the next however many years. Things will be hard enough for her with the twins and another baby on the way."

Doc looked shocked. "Susanne is pregnant?"

"Yes, but please act surprised when she tells us. She doesn't know that I know."

"I will," Doc said. "I will. I don't know what to say. First I find out that my son is going to die, and then I find out I'm going to be a grandpa again."

"Well, you know how it is: one soul leaves via the door marked 'exit' as one enters via the door marked 'entrance'."

Doc surprised himself by laughing. "Yes, I suppose so. Now we had better get back before they start to wonder what we're doing in here."

When they got back, Susanne looked at Val. "And just what have you two been up to in there?"

"Oh, nothing. It's just Doc complaining. He's bending my ear about not seeing enough of the twins."

"Well, I suppose we'll have to do something about that, won't we?" Susanne stood up. "Now that everyone is here, firstly I would like to say thank you to all of you for all the help and support you have given to Val and me through everything. Now for some good news. Val says that drilling holes in his head and implanting brains in there seems to have worked." Everyone laughed. "There is just one more thing I would like to say. This is something that not even Val knows yet." She paused. Everyone was looking at her. "We are going to have another baby."

There was a moment of silence, and then everyone cheered.

Val jumped up and grabbed her. "Really?" he said. "We're going to have another baby?"

"You're not angry, are you, that I waited to tell you and everyone else at the same time?"

"No, of course not. I want to say that I love you with all my heart."

Doc thought that maybe Val should have been an actor because he was certainly good at it. If he hadn't already known the truth, he would probably have believed him. Maybe Val was right. What was the point of worrying when nothing might happen? But he knew the answer to that: something would happen. It was just a case of when. Val was still the closest thing to a son he had. He had raised him from twelve years old, so it was going to be tough. Now it was as if Val was living under the sword of Damocles. All Doc could do was hope that the rope wouldn't break.

The atmosphere around the table was one of happiness. Val had accepted the job he'd been offered in the training section. He said that, with a wife and three kids to support, he didn't think that Susanne was going to be able to keep him in the style he had been hoping to become accustomed to. Everyone laughed. It was a good day.

+++

Val was happy working in the training section; he felt that it was where he should be, where he belonged. After Susanne gave birth to Ryan, she decided to give up her job and become a full-time mother. It was just after Ryan had been born that Miss Susanne Wilder became Mrs. Susanne Frankland. The wedding was a fantastic affair. Lewis and Lilly put on a superb wedding day for Val and Susanne, and the couple was very happy together.

Time passed, and Doc continued to watch and wait. He watched Val and Susanne raise their children. By the time the twins were twelve, Dexter looked so much like his dad it was amazing. To Doc, looking at Dexter was just like looking at Val when he was that age. Lilly was very much like, Susanne, and even at twelve, she had all the boys following her around. Ryan looked more like Susanne that Val, but the way he moved and his temperament was all Val. As small children, they would sit and watch Val as he did his workouts. This was not exactly karate or kung fu, but a mixture of many martial arts. Then they started to join in and learn. By the time the twins reached twelve and Ryan reached eleven, they were all more than a physical match for most people. If they worked together, they could even beat their dad. Doc reckoned it wouldn't be long before they were better than Val on one.

Of the three children, Ryan was the closest to his father. He moved, acted, and talked just like him. When he was doing his exercises, any onlooker might compare him to a cat. All three of the children took after Val in singing, dancing, and playing musical instruments. When they all played together, Doc reckoned they could have been professionals. For one of the songs they performed, Ryan played drums, Dexter played lead guitar, and Lilly played rhythm and sang. Val and Susanne always danced to this particular song; in fact, they said it was their song. Doc had a video of the family performance. He said it was the most beautiful song he had ever heard. It brought tears to his eyes, it was just so beautiful.

The years had been kind, and without realizing it, Doc had begun to relax and to think that maybe Val would be all right. After all, it had been a lot of years since that doctor had told Val he might only live a few more years—or days. Maybe Doc could afford to relax.

+++

One day just after the twins had turned sixteen, Lilly came home from school to find her dad sitting in the kitchen at the table. He had what looked like a letter in one hand, and he was rubbing his forehead with his other hand. "Hi, Dad. You're home early," she said.

"Hmm?" he said.

"I said you're home early. Are you all right?"

"Yes. Just a bit of a headache."

"Where's Mom?"

"She went to the grocery store. She'll be back soon." There was something in his voice that made Lilly look more closely at him.

"Are you sure you're all right?" she asked again.

Val raised his head to look at her. Lilly saw his face and screamed. She ran to him. His face was as white as chalk, his nose was bleeding, and there was blood running from his eyes. He looked like a scary clown. "Daddy! Daddy! What's happening?" Just then the front door opened. "Mom is that you?" Lilly screamed.

"No," Dexter said, running towards the kitchen. "It's me and Ryan. Why?"

"Help me!" she shouted. "For God's sake, help me!"

Both boys dropped their bags on the floor and hurried into the kitchen. "What's wrong?" asked Dexter.

"It's Dad. There's something wrong with Dad!"

Dexter and Ryan saw Val with the blood all over his face. "Oh my God," Dexter said. "Let's get him into the living room and onto the sofa."

Once they had got Val onto the sofa, Lilly knelt beside him and took his hand.

"Where's Mom?" Ryan asked.

"Dad said she was at the grocery store," said Lilly. "Ryan, you call an ambulance. Dexter, you call Mom and tell her we need her here now."

The boys did as Lilly had told them. She was still kneeling beside her father holding his hand telling him he would be all right and that Mom would be there soon.

Val looked at her. "Lilly-bee?" he said. "What are you doing here? Shouldn't you be in school?"

"Don't you worry, Dad. Mom will be here soon, so just you relax."

A few moments later the door burst open and Susanne rushed in. She saw Val laying on the sofa. "Oh, my God! Has someone called an ambulance?" she asked.

"Yes, Ryan did that," Lilly said.

"Has anyone called Grandpa?"

"No, not yet," Lilly said.

Susanne called him and told him what had happened. "An ambulance is on the way."

Right," Doc said. "I'll meet you at the hospital. I'll let Thomes and the others know."

"Thank you," Susanne said.

"Just remember he loves you, and I'm sure he'll be okay."

"We need to get him to hospital as soon as we can," the paramedic said.

"What is it?" Dexter asked the paramedic. "What's wrong with him?"

"When we get him to the hospital, they'll run some tests and then the doctors will be able to tell you more," the paramedic told him.

They all went with Val to the hospital. Susanne was sitting in the waiting room with her children around her when Thomes and the others arrived. "How is he?" Thomes asked.

"We don't know yet," Susanne said. "They're still running tests."

"Has anyone called my mom and dad?" Thomes asked.

"Yes, I spoke to Grandma Lilly," Lilly said. "She said she would tell Grandpa Lewis and they would get here as soon as they could." Lilly was pacing up and down. "It's this waiting that's the worst," she said.

The doctor came into the waiting room. "Mrs. Frankland?" he asked.

Susanne stood. "Yes, that's me."

"Could I have a private word with you please?"

"You can say what you have to say in front of these people. We're all family here."

"Very well. It might be better if you sit down. I'm afraid I have some bad news for you."

Susanne began to cry. "Is he dead?"

"No, he's still alive, but I'm afraid that he's gravely ill. I'm sorry to say that we found a large tumor in his brain, and I'm sorry to say it's inoperable. We could try to shrink it, but apart from that, there's not much we can do. If he had come to us earlier, we might have been able to do something."

"What do mean you earlier? How long has it been there?"

"Well, I would think that it must have been there when the surgery was done on his skull. It must have been visible then."

Susanne looked at Doc. "Did you know about this?" she asked.

Doc looked down. "I suspected, but I didn't know for sure."

"Why didn't you say something?"

"Because I wasn't sure. If I had said something, and then there was nothing ..."

"Does this have anything to do with me?" Ryan asked in a small voice.

Susanne turned to him. "Good God, no. Whatever would make you think that?"

The boy had tears in his eyes. "Remember when Dad was teaching us to fight and I wouldn't hit him? He kept saying that I was weak and that I would never be as good as Lilly or Dexter. That made me mad, and I hurt him. He laughed about it after. But could that have caused this?"

Susanne pulled him to her. "Oh, honey. No, you didn't cause this."

Dexter and Lilly put their arms around Susanne and Ryan. "This was caused by a man called Ricardo," Susanne told them. "He used to work with us on Uncle Dexter's team. We all worked together. Now, I knew that he liked me but not how much, but it didn't matter how much he liked me because your dad turned up one morning, and that was it."

"Love at first sight," Lilly said. "That is so magical."

"Yes, that's just what it was like," said Susanne. "It was magical, just as Lill-Bee said. But you see, I didn't realize just how jealous Ricardo was. He paid some guys to kill your dad, and when that failed, he paid a hospital orderly to poison your dad. That also went wrong, so he had me kidnapped to lure your dad into a trap. Then he shot him—twice once in the chest and once in the head."

"What happened to this Ricardo?" Ryan asked.

"Your Uncle Benny shot and killed him."

"Good deal," Dexter said.

"The bullet that hit your father hit at an angle so it ran down the side of his skull tearing a part of it away. So, what happened with you and your dad did not cause this, okay?" she reassured her son.

"Okay," Ryan said. "I was worried just in case it was."

"Well, you don't have to worry."

"I'm sorry about that, doctor," Susanne said to the doctor, who had been patiently listening. Please carry on with what you were saying."

"I was saying that I can try to shrink the tumor, but I don't know how effective that would be in a tumor this advanced."

Susanne thought back to when Val was in his coma. She remembered Thomes advising her to let him go with dignity because it was what he would have wanted.

"How long does he have?" Susanne asked.

"It's hard to say. Maybe six months? I am sorry."

"Can I take him home?" she asked.

"He will need a lot of care," the doctor said.

"That won't be a problem," she said.

"I'll prescribe some medication that should help, but as time goes on and his condition worsens, he may require round-the-clock care."

"That won't be a problem I'll arrange for nurses and anything else he needs."

"Very well, if that's what you want," the doctor said.

"Yes, it's what I want—what we all want. I think Val would also want this."

"Okay. We'll stabilize him and arrange for him to be transferred."

"Thank you very much. I'll make arrangements for him at home." Susanne began to cry. Dexter, Lilly, and Ryan gathered around her.

"Don't worry, Mom," Lilly said. "We'll help you. Everything will be okay. You'll see."

"Thank you," she said. "You are the best children a mother could wish for."

Thomes and the other members of his team stood around them. "If there's anything we can do—anything at all—just say it and we'll be there," he said.

"Thank you so much, all of you," said Susanne. "You have done so much for us. I don't know what I would have done without you over the years."

"Come on, Mom," Ryan said. "Let's go home now and get ready for Dad to come home."

+++

The next day, while they were making preparations for Val to come home, the doorbell rang. Susanne answered it to find a man standing there. Her children gathered behind her. She felt that she knew the man, but she didn't know where from. "Hello, can I help you?" she asked

"I hope so. I'm looking for Valentine Frankland." He spoke with an English accent.

"Who are you? And what do you want with Val?"

"I'm sorry. Where are my manners? My name is Hugh Frankland. Valentine Frankland is my nephew."

She stared at him for a moment. "You are Val's uncle? But Val has no family. How can you be his uncle?"

"My brother, Peter, was Val's father. He and Val's mother, Sarah, came to America when Val was only five. They were killed when a huge lorry crossed to their side of the road and collided with them. That was all I knew. I've been searching for Val for years, and I've finally tracked him here."

Susanne just looked at him saying nothing.

"Are you all right? You look a bit pale," Hugh said.

"Sorry, yes," she said. "It's just a bit of a shock. We always thought he had no family. *He* thought he had no family. I'm sorry. Please come in and sit down." Hugh followed her into the house where they all sat in the living room. "I'm Susanne, his wife, and these are our children. This is Dexter and Lilly, the twins, and this is Ryan." They shook hands all round. "This is Hugh Frankland, your father's uncle—your great-uncle."

"Uncle?" Dexter asked. "I thought dad had no family."

"We didn't know what had happened to Peter, Sarah, and Val for the first few years," explained Hugh. "When we found out that Peter and Sarah had been killed, we tried to find Val, but without any luck. I wrote to every government agency I could find trying to find out what had happened to Val, but I always got the same reply. There was no record of Valentine Frankland. I kept on trying. Then, just by chance, I found a record for the marriage of Valentine Frankland to Susanne Wilder. It was the only Frankland I found, so I thought it must be him, and I knew I had to find him. It has taken me until now, but at last, I am here."

Susanne and the children just sat looking at him. "When I first opened the door," Susanne told him, "I thought I knew you from somewhere, and now I know why. You look a bit like Val. I'm very sorry to tell you this, but you have arrived a little late."

"How do you mean a little late?"

"They have discovered a tumor in Val's brain." Susanne began to cry again. "They don't think he has very long to live."

Susanne watched the man's entire body sag. "Might I ask if I could visit him? The last time I saw him, he was only four years old, and I was so looking forward to seeing him again after all these years." He reached into the inside pocket and took out a photo. "This is a photo of Val the last time I saw him. He's with his mom and dad." He handed the photo to Susanne.

"Oh, my God," she said. "That could be Val *or* Dexter!" The children looked over their mom's shoulder at the picture.

"I'll be returning to England soon," said Hugh. "But I would like to see Val once before I leave."

"Of course. Val will be coming home soon. We have decided that he would be happier at home. If you would like to visit him here, that might be better than the hospital."

"Thank you. Thank you so much," he said.

"Can I ask you something?" Susanne said.

"I know what you want to ask. And the answer is yes, Val does have more family. My wife and I have four children, all of then grown with their children. Then there is his mother's side of the family. So, you see, he has lots of families, or should I say you all have lots of families. They will be so excited when I tell them about all of you."

"Do you know why my dad and his parents came over here in the first place?" Dexter asked.

Hugh smiled. "That was the cause of the argument between Peter and me. Both he and Sarah worked for the British government doing some top-secret work. Then one day Peter said they were coming over here to work for the American government. I think their work was the reason it took so long for us to find out that they had been killed in that accident, and because of that, I lost the chance to find Val."

"So, you had no idea what happened to Val?" Susanne said.

"No. I was hoping that Val would be able to tell me all about it."

"I can tell you a lot of what happened to him beginning from the time he was seven years old."

Susanne brewed a pot of coffee and then told Hugh the story, as Doc had told her, about how Val had been fostered out. She went on to explain how Doc had found him and raised him as his own. She told him about his marriage to Juliet, and her death, and about how Val was torn apart by that. She told him about Val's time in the army and his government work. Finally, she told him how they had met and fallen in love. "Although one of our team tried several times to kill him," she finished, "we married and started our own family."

"Well, that's quite a story, and it finally explains why I could never find him. But he has certainly had an eventful life, and he is a very lucky man. He has a very beautiful wife and three wonderful children."

"Thank you. Val will be coming home in a few days. If you want to, you can come and visit him then."

"Thank you. I would like that very much."

"If you leave me a contact number I'll call you when he's home and settled."

"Thank you very much," he said again. He gave Susanne his number and left.

"What do you think your father will say when we tell him?"

"I think he'll be so excited," Ryan said. "Just think—we have a family we never knew existed. Maybe we could go visit them when Dad gets better."

Susanne smiled. "Yes, I think that would be lovely. I think your dad would like that."

+++

A few days later, Susanne and the children brought Val home. They made him as comfortable as possible. Susanne called Hugh, as she had promised, and he came to visit Val. He introduced himself, and the two men talked. Hugh told Val about all the family he had in England and how he had tried for so long to find Val after the accident that had killed his parents. Val talked about his life after the accident.

Susanne was happy that Hugh had found Val and they had the chance to meet and talk. Phone numbers were exchanged, photos were taken, and existing photos exchanged. Hugh said he had to return to England, but he would be in touch again as soon as he could.

Melanie, Benny, Trena, Doc, and Thomes called to visit Val as often as they could. Melanie had married Benny, and they had their own family, but they spent as much time as they could with Val. All of the children spent a lot of time with their dad, but Ryan seemed to spend most of his spare time with his dad. When Val was awake, Ryan would sit and talk to him, and when he was asleep, he would just sit with him.

The first time Doc called in to see how Val was doing, Susanne had told him about Hugh and his visit to meet Val and about Hugh's search for Val. She had told about the news of Val's family in England.

"And he always thought he was alone," said Doc when he heard the news. "Does he know? Have you told him?"

"Yes. Hugh told him. I told him as well, but I don't know if he took it all in at the time. I'll tell him again later." Susanne told him that Hugh had returned to England, but that he'd promised to keep in touch and come back as soon as he could.

"How is Val holding up?"

"He has his good days and his bad days. Ryan seems to spend much of his time just sitting there talking to him."

"Remind you of anyone?" Doc asked smiling.

She smiled wanly. "What am I going to do without him?"

"We have to be strong. We must never give up hope. Do you mind if I sit with him for a while?"

"No, not at all. If he wakes up, he'll like that."

Doc sat just looking at Val. He thought of all the good times there had been. And now, how wonderful it was for Val to find out that he had family in England. Perhaps if they had found that out back then, none of this would ever have happened. Maybe he would have lived a longer, happier life, but then again, maybe not. That was something they would never know.

CHAPTER 18

Goodbye, My Love

Doc was sitting at Val's bedside. Thoughts about what had happened all those years ago were going through his mind. He looked at Val. Why had he let things get to this point? Maybe he should have said something back then.

Val woke to see Doc sitting beside him. "Hey there. Nice to see you, Pops."

"You haven't called me that in a long time."

Val could see the tears in the old man's eyes. He reached out and took Doc's hand. "Don't beat yourself up over this. You are not to blame."

"Maybe if I had told someone back then?"

"No, you did the right thing not telling Susanne or anyone else for that matter. If you had told them, it wouldn't have changed anything, and you know that. I've had a lot of good years with Susanne, and I have three wonderful children. What more could any man ask for?"

"But it's not right," Doc said.

"Listen to me. I'm going to tell you something. People say 'Oh, poor Val, what a hard time he's had—all alone as a child, and he's been alone since.' Now I admit, at first after my parents got killed, it was difficult. But then you found me. You took me in and raised me as your child. Then I met Thomes and Juliet, Lewis and Lilly. Later I met Susanne, along with Melanie and Trena and even Benny, so I had a large family that has always been there for me. And then, to put the icing on the cake, my uncle showed up from England and told me that I have an even bigger family than I thought!"

Doc looked at Val. "What?" Val asked. "What is it?"

"You remember it all."

"Yes, I remember everything."

"How long have you had your memory back?"

"Ever since they drilled holes in my head."

"Why didn't you say anything to us?"

"There didn't seem to be any point. What good would it have done? Everything that I had forgotten and then remembered was in the past and had no place in my future."

"And we all thought you couldn't remember any of it."

Val smiled at him. "I want to thank you for all the help, love and care you gave me as a child. And for never giving up on me. I wish that I had the time to thank all the others as well, but I don't think that's going to happen."

"Don't say that. You have plenty of time. There are lots of things we still have to do. We have to visit your family in England for one thing."

"Sorry, Pops, but I think my time has just about run out. Remember, don't be thinking 'if I'd done this' or 'if I'd done that'. Nothing would have made a difference. It wouldn't. From the moment Ricardo pulled that trigger and his bullet entered my head, there was no changing anything. I'm feeling a little tired now. Would you call Susanne for me please?"

"Yes, of course."

"Always remember that I love you, Dad."

Doc called Susanne and left her with Val. "What was all that about?" Susanne asked her husband.

Val touched his head. "He's blaming himself for this."

Susanne started to say something, but Val took her hand and stopped her. "Listen, there is something I have to say to you. I love you so much, and the years that we have been together have been the best years of my life. Every day I felt as if I was falling in love with you over again. It was like seeing the world for the first time every day. I do love you so very much, and I don't want to leave you."

"Leave me? What do you mean, leave me? You're not going any-where. You're staying here with us."

"I'm sorry, my love, but I don't think I have any choice in the matter. Not this time. I do want to say thank you for loving me and for the three beautiful children you gave me."

"No, you can't go! I need you here. We need you here. You can't leave us."

He reached up and touched her cheek. He wiped away a tear. "You are so very beautiful, and I have been so very lucky that you have loved me. Please say goodbye to the children for me. Tell them all that I love them so much and that they have to be strong."

"No," she said again. "You can't go! You can't leave us. We love you. We need you—*I* need you!"

Val looked up into her face. "Susanne," he said.

"Yes, my love," she said through her tears.

"I'm scared," he said. He exhaled, and his hand fell away from her face. Then he simply didn't take another breath.

"No!" Susanne cried. "No! You can't go! It's not fair I need you. Come back!"

Doc came into the room and put his hand on her shoulder. "Susanne," he said.

She didn't look around; she didn't answer. She just lay across Val and cried. "Don't be scared," she said softly. "Don't be scared, my love. I will be with you always and forever."

+++

Susanne stood alone by the angel memorial and the rose bush that marked the place where Val's ashes had been scattered. She was crying. Why was she there still wearing her nightgown? She was not afraid. She knew that Val loved her and would never have done anything to hurt her when he was alive, and she knew that he wouldn't hurt her now.

She felt his hand stroke the side of her face. She gasped. Then she heard his voice just as clearly as if he were standing there right behind her. "I hope you're not going to be a crybaby," he said, and he laughed. Then he was gone.

"Val?" she cried. "Val?" She woke up shouting his name over and over. Tears were streaming down her cheeks.

Lilly, Dexter, and Ryan rushed into her bedroom. They found her crying, sitting up in the middle of the bed with all the bedclothes pooled round her.

"What is it?" Lilly asked. "What's wrong?"

"It was just a dream. Just a dream."

"Was it about Dad?" Ryan asked.

"Yes, it was. It was."

"Did he tell you not to be a crybaby?" Ryan asked.

Susanne looked at him with her mouth open. "Yes, he did. But how can you have known that?"

"Because I saw him in my dream as well."

"When was that?" she asked.

"I was dreaming just before you woke me up shouting his name. He looked like he did before …" Ryan looked down. "Before, you know …"

"Yes, I know," she said. She kissed his forehead.

Ryan smiled. "He hugged me and told me to be brave. He said that I should look after you and tell you not to be a crybaby."

"I saw him as well," Dexter said. "And it was like Ryan said—he hugged me and told me to take care of you."

"It was the same for me," Lilly said. "But what does it mean?"

"I think it means he wants us to be happy and that he will always be with us."

"But I don't understand why he told us all to tell you not to be a crybaby," Lilly said.

Susanne smiled as she thought about it. "When we first met, and Ricardo was doing his best to kill your father, it seemed that I was always crying. Your father used to say 'I hope you're not going to be a crybaby when we're married.' And here I am again crying."

They all sat together on Susanne's bed.

"Why did he have to go?" Ryan said. "I miss him."

Susanne stroked Ryan's hair. "I know you do. We all miss him, but he will never really be gone from us. As long as we hold him in our hearts, he will never truly be gone. Not really. He will live within each of us." Susanne pulled her three children close to her. "We will always have each other, and we will have the closest of friends."